5/26

The Bible Salesman

———

The Bible Salesman

A NOVEL

Clyde Edgerton

LITTLE, BROWN AND COMPANY
New York   Boston   London

Copyright © 2008 by Clyde Edgerton

Little, Brown and Company
Hachette Book Group USA
237 Park Avenue, New York, NY 10017
Visit our Web site at www.HachetteBookGroupUSA.com

First Edition: August 2008

Little, Brown and Company is a division of Hachette Book Group USA, Inc. The Little, Brown logo is a trademark of Hachette Book Group USA, Inc.

The characters and events in this book are fictitious. Any similarity to real persons, living or dead, is coincidental and not intended by the author.

Excerpts from *The Complete Bible: An American Translation*, translated by J. M. Powis Smith and Edgar J. Goodspeed, are reprinted by permission. Copyright © 1923, 1927, 1948 by the University of Chicago.

Library of Congress Cataloging-in-Publication Data
Edgerton, Clyde.
    The Bible salesman : a novel / Clyde Edgerton. — 1st ed.
        p.   cm.
    ISBN-13: 978-0-316-11751-7
    ISBN-10: 0-316-11751-X
    1. Automobile thieves — Fiction. 2. Teenage boys — Fiction. 3. North Carolina — Fiction. 4. United States — History — 1945–1953 — Fiction. I. Title.
PS3555.D47B53   2008
813'.54 — dc22   2007045410

10 9 8 7 6 5 4 3 2 1

RRD-IN

Book design by Fearn Cutler de Vicq
Printed in the United States of America

For Kristina, forever

Contents

AUTHOR'S NOTE

Apparent usage irregularities in some characters' speech are controlled by grammatical rules — just as in standard English. This is true of dialects the world over. Since language is not normally spoken in a vacuum, but rather in situations among people, it is clear and reasonable that the use of language be judged by custom and appropriateness rather than by principles of "correctness" drawn from mathlike assumptions.

Biblical quotations, unless otherwise noted in the narrative, are from the King James Version.

PART I

EXODUS

1950

———

A man driving a new Chrysler automobile along a dirt road near the North Carolina mountain town of Cressler saw a boy up ahead, dressed in a black suit, white shirt, black tie, with a suitcase and valise by his feet. The boy was standing in front of a grocery store, thumbing a ride.

The man, working his way up, belonged to a crime outfit. He was now at the car-theft level, hungry for wealth and the tense excitement he found nowhere outside crime.

The boy was a twenty-year-old Bible salesman whose aunt raised him to be a Christian gentleman. He was hungry for adventure and good food. He had recently started reading the Bible on his own rather than as directed by his aunt and church elders, and he hadn't been able to get past those first two chapters of Genesis — because they amazed and confused him.

The man thought he recognized something smart and businesslike in the boy's stance — almost at attention — and he also sensed some gullibility and innocence. His last associate had not worked out. He slowed and pulled over in the rising dust. If this one didn't seem promising, he'd just let him out down the road.

The boy loaded his things into the backseat, closed the back door, bent his head forward, and folded into the front passenger seat. The man noticed the boy's leftover belt end hanging down freely without being put through the first loop, his hair standing up on top in back. Maybe he *won't* so smart.

"Nice car," said the boy. " 'Fifty Chrysler." He reached out his hand. "I'm Henry Dampier." Henry was surprised at the man's big hand. And he had big ears. He looked a little bit like Clark Gable, but without a mustache.

"Preston Clearwater," said the man. "Where you headed?"

"Anywhere south. Where it's a little warmer. I came up here earlier than I ought to have." The man was dressed up neat, and he'd shaved real close that morning, it looked like. He'd have a dark beard if he grew it out. He was wearing cuff links, and Henry had never seen those except at a prom.

"I'm selling Bibles," said Henry. "But it's too cold sleeping in warehouses and barns up in this high altitude." He noticed how smoothly the car glided over the dirt road. "Where *you* headed?"

"Winston-Salem, or maybe Charlotte — for tonight, anyway."

The night before, Henry had sat up late in a deserted warehouse razoring out the front pages of new Bibles that had arrived in Cressler, general delivery — from Chicago — in a cardboard box. Each page said, "Complimentary Copy from the Chicago Bible Society."

Henry looked at Mr. Clearwater's hands. They were clean. "What line of work you in?"

None of your goddamned business, thought Clearwater. "Car business," he said. He pulled out a pack of Luckies, shook up a couple. "Cigarette?"

"Sure." Henry had bought his first-ever pack of cigarettes only a few days earlier.

Clearwater pushed in the cigarette lighter. "Where you get your Bibles?"

"Where do I get my Bibles?" Henry looked at him. Could he *know* somehow? "That's kind of a long story." He did want to tell about it — this idea he got from the fiddle player at Indian Springs in Cressler: instead of ordering Bibles and having to pay, why didn't he just go ahead and order a box from one of those places up north, or in Nashville, Tennessee, maybe, that gave away Bibles, tell them he had a bunch of sinners to give them to, razor out the pages that said they're free, and sell them? The fiddle player said he'd had that idea when he thought about selling Bibles himself, but gave it up when his wife had twins and his mama died. Henry had wondered if he was kidding, but took the idea anyway.

So Henry had been ordering a box of free Bibles about once a month, each from a different place so that nobody got suspicious. In the letter to them he kind of hinted that he was a preacher. But nobody got hurt, and in the end more people ended up reading the Bible, which was good, and now his billfold, his spare billfold — stashed in his suitcase — was considerably thick with money, somewhere between forty and fifty dollars, and some uncashed checks. He could go ahead and stay in a decent room for a change. And now here he was riding in a brand-new Chrysler. With a man who looked like he knew how to do things out in the world.

"This smells like a new car too," said Henry.

"It's pretty new."

Henry noticed the ivory-looking knob on the end of the gearshift — he couldn't quite see the top speed on the speed-ometer. "Six or eight?" he asked.

"Eight. Hundred and thirty-five horsepower."

"That's pretty good. So, do you *sell* cars?"

"Yeah." Clearwater, with his lips closed, passed his tongue over his front teeth. "I do that."

Henry figured he'd be quiet, give Mr. Clearwater a chance to kind of talk or not talk. He didn't want to chitchat him-self into getting dropped off somewhere.

"Where you from?" asked Clearwater.

"Simmons, North Carolina. Down east."

"Is that anywhere close to McNeill and Swan Island?"

"About an hour or so. I went there a few times when I was growing up."

"I know some people there. Mitchells."

"I don't know any Mitchells down there. My uncle took us all there one time — me and my sister and aunt — to see this big dance hall that was one of the first places in North Carolina that used electricity fancylike. They showed movies on a screen set up in the surf."

"I heard about that."

Clearwater's boss, Blinky, owned a warehouse in McNeill that held some stolen army equipment. It was part of Blinky's cover — a business called Johnson and Ball Construction and Industrial Machine Repair Company.

The drive to Winston-Salem would take three or four hours. Clearwater began to feel Henry out, learned that he was raised by his aunt and uncle. That his daddy got killed right after Henry was born, hit by a piece of timber sticking out from the back of a moving truck. That he was a Christian. That he liked baseball and had played on a church team coached by two men who worked at a funeral home and used baby caskets to hold the bases and other equipment. That he went to Bible-selling school instead of business school and was taught to sell Bibles by a man who walked back and forth in front of the class, chain-smoking cigarettes and coughing and telling funny stories. That he had an older sister named Caroline and an uncle he liked to talk about — Uncle Jack. And a cousin — Carson. And though Henry didn't say it, Clearwater could sense he was a virgin, because of how he'd talked around some stuff about women. That was good — it'd help both of them stay out of woman trouble if he did hire him.

He also found out the boy knew when to shut up — when

Clearwater was talking. Damned important. And he seemed to have an adequate sense of adventure without a too-big portion of carelessness. In fact, Clearwater felt a little bit lucky to have found this Henry Dampier.

Along about Wilkesboro, down out of the real mountains and into hilly country, Clearwater pulled over, stopped, and asked Henry to drive.

The boy was clearly happy to be behind the wheel of a car, and he was a good driver, kept his eye on the road, didn't go too fast, drove around holes. Clearwater talked some about his own service in the army, in France. He didn't tell Henry he'd met Blinky there and that they — with creative paperwork and bold presentations of self — managed to steal two dump trucks, a forklift, four jeeps, seven chain saws, and sixteen hundred pairs of aviator sunglasses. Blinky had them shipped to a warehouse in McNeill owned by his Aunt Thelma, the nonsuspecting wife of his dead uncle, Gabe Mitchell. He told Henry he'd been to business school, but he didn't tell him that that had slowed him down and left him behind Blinky in the crime business — and now he was trying to catch up. He told him some stuff about his communist mama, who believed in Jesus. She believed the Indians were communists and that Jesus was a communist. Course you couldn't talk about the communists now without somebody thinking you were one, Clearwater said, like he always said when he talked about his mama. And this Henry Dampier knew something about the Russians and Chinese and the atom bomb, more than he could say about some of the potential associates he'd come across since he'd turned loose his last one. And even though all that was true about Clearwater's mama, a lot of people didn't believe it, but this one seemed like he did, so Clearwater reckoned he was maybe gullible enough.

They stopped in Winston-Salem in the late afternoon, at the Sanderson Motel. Clearwater would pick up some "sheets" there — information, leads, suggested marks. He had a route that took him throughout the South, like any other traveling businessman.

"I need to do some work in town," said Clearwater. "You go on in and get a room. It's best if I don't appear to be traveling with anybody. I can explain at breakfast. Right over there at Mae's." Mae's had a big yellow sign on top of a small café. "I have a job available you might want. I'll see you over there at seven-thirty?"

"Yes sir."

Blinky, from his cover — the Johnson and Ball Company in McNeill — provided the sheets. Most of his leads required reconnaissance, some required planning, and all thefts were to be reported.

Clearwater researched and planned carefully. During the next day or two he'd find a mark, make maps, decide alibis, and plan exactly how to use his new associate, if the boy took the job. An associate would certainly reduce his chances of getting caught.

The motel clerk, a little man with thick glasses, gave Henry a key and a flyswatter. On the counter was a wire display rack holding postcards, a color photograph of the motel on the front of each. Henry bought two. Displayed under a glass countertop were necklaces, rings, and packs of exotic cards.

"How much is a pack of those cards?"

"Twenty-five cents. I got some under the counter for fifty cents. Want to take a look?"

"Maybe tomorrow. I'll take that twenty-five-cent pack, though."

In his room, Henry put his suitcase in a corner and his valise on the bed. An electric lamp made from an oil lamp stood on a chest of drawers beside a radio. He noticed three cigarette burns along the edge of the chest top. Some burns had been sanded off, it looked like. He hung his suit and his sport coat on a wire hanger in the small closet, took off his shirt and undershirt and dropped them in a corner. He'd wash them in the tub, do some ironing if they had an iron in the office. He looked in each dresser drawer. Top: empty. Middle: a book of matches. He pocketed it. Bottom: empty.

This prospect with Mr. Clearwater could get him into something a little higher up — well, not out of Bible selling altogether; he didn't want that. He could keep selling Bibles on weekends, at least.

A full-length mirror leaned against the wall beside the dresser, bottom left corner broken off. He dropped his boxer shorts, kicked them into the corner, turned sideways, drew in his stomach, expanded his chest, clinched his fist, hardened his arm muscles. He turned and faced the mirror, crossed his arms. He turned his head left, right. Checked his hangings. They always looked bigger in a mirror than when you looked down.

He stopped up the tub drain with the chained stopper and let the water run longer than he ever did at home. Aunt Dorie let him use only just enough water to reach the back of the tub. He stepped in and sat slowly. The water was hot. It had been almost two weeks since he'd had a shower at a barbershop. He slid down so his head rested against the back of the tub and closed his eyes. He thought about this possible new job. Mr. Clearwater looked like he made a lot of money.

He wet and then soaped his head, neck, arms, under his arms, his chest and back, pushed his midsection up out of the water, soaped his hangings and the crack of his ass. He then slid down into the water, pushing his knees up, splashed water over his chest. He stuck fingers in his ears, dropped his head back into the water, held it there and shook it to rinse his hair. He sat up. The water was gray. He splashed water over himself some more, stood, stepped out onto a small, round rug, dried himself with the towel, wrapped it around his waist, walked back to the standing mirror, and looked at himself again.

He dressed in clean clothes from his suitcase. The white shirt was wrinkled, but the pants weren't too bad. He buckled his belt. He found his long black comb in the inside flap of his suitcase and combed his hair back while standing in front of the full-length mirror. Back at the sink he wet the washcloth, wrung it out, and smoothed down his hair. Like Uncle Jack.

What kind of job might it be? Anybody driving a new Chrysler could probably pay a good salary — or worked for somebody who could.

It was four o'clock, not too late to sell a Bible or two and maybe get invited somewhere for supper. He walked north along the road to a row of houses he'd seen from the motel office. He carried his valise and, in his head, lessons from Mr. Fletcher.

My job is to teach you how to sell Bibles, gentlemen. Period. End of story. From an economic point of view there are two and only two sides to every customer encounter: making the sale or not making the sale. Economics is the invisible hand that moves the world. So: two sides — the head, the tail; a sale, no sale. Kaput. The end. And you will squeeze every opportunity out of every moment of every customer encounter to make that sale. So now, gentlemen. Let's start by writing down a definition of Bible selling. Bible selling . . . is the act . . . of getting customers . . . to behave in ways . . . assumed . . . to lead to . . . Bible buying. Bible selling is the act of getting customers to behave in ways assumed to lead to Bible buying. Let's all read it together now, and then you'll memorize it, and I can promise you it will be one of the last statements you remember as you pass from this mortal realm into the next. Bible selling is the act of . . .

He walked past three houses that didn't look inviting — dirt yards. Except one of the yards was raked. Next, after a short stretch of woods, three houses with lawns and shrubs sat back a ways from the road. He checked in his valise to be sure the Bibles were arranged, pulled out the box containing a Bible, walked up and knocked on the screen door. He heard steps. The inside door opened and a woman stood holding a cooking pot and a drying rag.

"How do you do, ma'am? My name is Henry Dampier, and I have a little something in this box that is mighty nice that I'd like to show you if you don't mind. It's something I think you might like — if I could step inside for a minute, maybe."

"I appreciate it, but I ain't interested in buying nothing today. My cat died this morning. I'm behind on everything. I just got to washing and drying my dinner dishes."

"Oh, mercy. That cat was probably just like a member of the family."

"She was. She sure was." The woman stood without moving, not much life in her face, her eyes.

You do __not__ want to keep standing out there on the porch with the screen door between y'all. You want to get inside, and you do that by looking and talking in ways to make her like you in about ten seconds — that's all you got.

"Oh Lord," said Henry. "I remember when we buried Trixie, my uncle's dog. It was all tears around the house when Trixie died. My sister especially. What was your cat's name, ma'am?"

"Bunny. I called her Bunny Rabbit."

He saw that her hand which had been against the door screen was still there. "I'm awful sorry. Did I introduce myself?" It was a matter of seconds now.

"You did, but I done forgot your name."

"Henry Dampier, ma'am. I tell you what, ma'am. Have you buried Bunny yet?"

"No, I ain't been able to bring myself to do it. Burt — Burt's my husband — he'll do it when he gets home."

"I was going to offer to say a little prayer at Bunny's grave."

Sometimes, gentlemen, you'll need to improvise. Jazz musicians do that when they put new notes where a melody used to be. They get off the beaten path, but brilliantwise.

"I'd be happy," said Henry, "just to step around back and bury her, if you got a shovel. I'm very partial to cats."

"Oh, that would be real nice, Mr. Dampier." She stepped out onto the porch. "I been here by myself, and I just couldn't bring myself to do it, so I was going to wait until Burt got home. Bunny's under the back steps." They were slowly moving toward the porch steps.

"If you want to," said Henry, "you can stay in the house and I'll do it, if you'll tell me a good place for a grave. I don't believe I got your name — not that I really need to, but it's always —"

"I'm Martha Kelly." She reached out her hand, and Henry took it. "Well, that would be real nice," she said. "You can see her rear end out from under the steps. I just couldn't bring myself to . . . She's over fifteen years old. Anywhere out in the edge of the woods would be good — straight back beyond the middle apple tree back there. The shovel is leaning against the back of the house. Lord, it's been a blue, blue day. She was like a, well, like a child. Just . . . just knock on the back door when you're finished. Oh my goodness. Poor Bunny. Poor Bunny."

"I'll just leave my valise right here on the porch," said Henry, "and my little box."

I'm here to tell you that there is one thing more important than sickness and health, life and death, love and war, food and water, and that is the sale. The sale. Understand that, if you want to sell a lot of Bibles. And you're hanging on to that possibility that you are leading her in the direction of her own behavior that's going to lead to her buying a Bible, and you won't turn loose without a sale, see, until you see clearly that you risk either getting killed or embarrassing yourself into stupidity.

"What are you selling?"

"I'm selling Bibles, ma'am. God's holy word."

Bunny's rear end was like she said: out from under the steps. Yellow. Henry couldn't see her head. He grabbed both back feet and pulled so she'd slide out. First he noticed the head was swollen way, *way* up. It was gigantic. Then he saw a . . . a snake — "Oh my gosh." He turned the cat loose and stepped back. The snake was hanging from her mouth, not moving — clearly dead too. "Oh my gosh." It was a copperhead, a small one. He squatted to examine. Somehow the snake's head . . . He looked around, picked up a rock and a short stick, wedged them into Bunny's mouth. Her front right big tooth was through the middle of the snake's head, and the snake's fangs were in Bunny's — what? — *lip,* which was twisted somehow. Oh my goodness, get them buried before the lady sees, he thought. She would die. That head was big as . . . big as a cantaloupe.

He looked into the neighbors' backyards. Nobody out there to see. He got the shovel underneath Bunny's midsection, lifted her — she was stiffening — and with the snake dangling, he started to the woods, his body between Bunny and the back door of the house. The snake, a little less than two feet long, held.

Just inside the tree line, beyond the middle apple tree, he lowered Bunny and the snake to the ground, dug a hole about two feet deep and plenty long — it was nice soft topsoil, no clay — and buried them. He patted the pile of dirt with the shovel. He thought about a cross, looked around for a big rock, found one, placed it at the head of the grave. That was one awful-looking cat head. Poor Bunny.

He stepped out of the woods and saw Mrs. Kelly coming, from just beyond the apple tree. As they met, he saw that her eyes were red.

"I can't tell you how much I appreciate this, Mr. Dampier." She held a tissue in her hand. "She hadn't been hit by a car, had she?"

"Oh no. No ma'am."

"When I went out to put water in her pan I saw her poor rear end and called and she didn't move, and I knew in my heart that that was the end. I think she died in her sleep, peacefully."

"Yes ma'am. That's what it was. That's what it looked like."

"I was worried she might, you know, have been hurt somehow." She looked over his shoulder toward the grave. "I lost my brother, Walter, in the war, and I haven't been able to deal with things very well since then. I have these nightmares. He was my only brother and . . . Were her eyes closed? That's one thing I always worry about."

"Oh yes ma'am. They were real closed."

"Would you show me the grave — walk with me out there?"

"Be glad to."

They stood at the foot of the grave. Henry tried to think of something to say. "I'll say a little prayer if you like," he said.

"Oh, that would be nice," said Mrs. Kelly.

They bowed their heads. Henry prayed, "Dear Lord, for the long life of Bunny we are grateful, and surely goodness and mercy has followed her all the days of her long life, and now she shall dwell in the house . . . or close to the house of the Lord forever. Amen."

"Amen," said Mrs. Kelly. "I always heard animals don't go to heaven," she said. "I was a Catholic when I was growing up, and that's what I always heard."

"That's what I always heard too, and I'm a Baptist, so I said 'close to' instead of 'in' for some reason. I don't know.

It's . . . you never know." Henry started moving away from the grave, back toward the house — he took a step or two.

But Mrs. Kelly stayed put. "I been thinking I ought to of had her buried *in* something," she said.

"You mean . . . you mean like a *dress?*" asked Henry. He saw a little dress with that giant head sticking up out of it. Bunny would need a *man's* hat.

"Oh no, like a shoe box or something. I just don't . . . I could get the box Burt's work boots come in. That hard cardboard would be fine to keep the dirt off her."

"You want to *re*bury her?"

"Yes." She looked up at Henry. "If you would. I want to see her again, one last time. I should have at least looked at her. I never got to see Walter. He had some kind of head injury, and none of us got to see him." She brought her tissue up to her eye. Then she started crying for sure and dropped to one knee. "Oh, Bunny. My beautiful Bunny."

Henry, holding the shovel, eyed the back of her house, where'd he'd planned to set the shovel back. He stood still, feeling some heat around his neck. Maybe he could sing something. *My Bunny lies over the ocean? My Bunny lies over the sea?* "I remember Trixie," he said, "this dog my uncle had. We just dropped her in a big hole and then threw the dirt in right on top of her. Never thought about a box. I think just plain dirt is the more or less normal way for an animal."

Mrs. Kelly, sniffing, said, "It's not too deep, is it? It wouldn't be a great bother to dig her back up, would it?"

"Oh, well, no, no ma'am. It's not too deep."

"If you don't mind," said Mrs. Kelly. "I'll go get the shoe box." She stood and started for the house.

Henry looked at the grave. No choice now. He started digging. Something would come to him. Improvise. He lifted Bunny on the shovel out of the grave. If I get rid of the snake maybe I can make up something, he thought. He thought about her brother, Walter. He looked toward the house. Mrs. Kelly was coming down the back steps with the box. He didn't want to get venom on his hand. He pulled out his handkerchief and, using it as a glove, pried Bunny's mouth open, pulled the snake's head off the tooth, looked up at Mrs. Kelly, her head down. She was almost to the apple tree. He flung the snake. The cat's head was enormous, the lips misshapen and bloody at the snake bite. The eyes — where in hell were the eyes? He tied his handkerchief around Bunny's head. He arranged the cloth, tucked.

Mrs. Kelly was standing there with the box.

"I'm just arranging a burial shroud," he said. "It's the way they bury all cats in England nowadays. I was just reading about it. It's a custom over there. Catching on here. I've done a few before."

"Her head looks swolled up."

"Oh no ma'am. That's from the way I arranged the handkerchief. Let me see that box. Poor thing." He almost snatched the box and, moving fast, put himself between Mrs. Kelly and Bunny, slipped Bunny in the box headfirst, shut the lid, and said, "Let's close our eyes in prayer. Our Heavenly Father, as we gather here, let us realize that Bunny has paid the final price, has reached her final destination, her final resting place" — he had one eye open and was moving the box into the hole with his foot — "and is now prepared for the kind of privacy that comes to all of us who have breathed our last breath after a faithful time of service of loving our masters, amen, and now I'm just going to pick up the shovel and cover her up with some mother earth and —"

"Her head looked swolled up to me."

"Oh no ma'am, it was the way you tuck a burial shroud that made it look that way. It's a kind of protection. It's called a burial tuck." Henry shoveled dirt onto the box. It made a sound like hard rain, and then the box was out of sight. If she said to uncover it, he would have to just walk off, he figured. Tell her he had to be somewhere.

"I can't thank you enough, Mr. Dampier," she said. "Burt will be home about suppertime. If you'll come back by, I'm sure he'll want to buy a Bible."

"I need to get on now, Mrs. Kelly, and what I'm going to do is give you a, a couple of Bibles. You've been through a lot today. I like to give away a complimentary Bible now and then, and I think you deserve a couple. Let's go pick them out." He patted the top of Bunny's grave a few times with the shovel, leaving imprints.

Back at the motel Henry noticed that Mr. Clearwater's car was gone. He ate supper across the street at Mae's — a patty of ground beef with mashed potatoes, biscuits, and string beans. Back in his motel room, he undressed and put on his pajamas. He knelt by his bed and prayed. "Dear God, help me to make the right decision in all I decide to do. Guide and direct me in the right path, oh God. In Jesus' name. Amen." He thought about Bunny, that head.

He sat on his bed and opened his Bible to Genesis. He read again, kind of fast, the first two chapters, then went back to the places he'd underlined. Aunt Dorie used to underline a lot in her Bible.

> In the beginning God created the heaven and the earth.
> And the earth was without form, and void; and
> darkness was upon the face of the deep. And the Spirit
> of God moved upon the face of the waters.

Then God made light, Henry read, and heaven, and earth, and plants by the third day. Then he made the seasons and sun and moon and stars on the fourth day. Then he made all the animals and creatures on the fifth day. He'd underlined "all the animals" and "fifth." He kept reading:

> And God said, Let us make man in our image, after
> our likeness: and let them have dominion over the fish
> of the sea, and over the fowl of the air, and over the
> cattle, and over all the earth, and over every creeping
> thing that creepeth upon the earth.
> So God created man in his own image, in the image
> of God created he him; male and female created he

them. And God blessed them. . . . <u>And the evening and</u> <u>the morning were the sixth day.</u>

<u>Thus the heavens and the earth were finished.</u>

So it was the sun, then animals, then people. *But then later,* in Genesis 2:

<u>And the LORD God formed man of the dust of the</u> <u>ground, and breathed into his nostrils the breath of</u> <u>life; and man became a living soul.</u>

And the LORD God planted a garden eastward in Eden; and there he put the man whom he had formed. . . .

And the LORD God said, It is not good that the man should be alone; I will make him an help meet for him. <u>And out of the ground the LORD God formed every</u> <u>beast of the field, and every fowl of the air; and</u> <u>brought them unto Adam to see what he would call</u> <u>them.</u>

First way: animals, then people. Second way: people, then animals.

Nobody had ever talked to him about two completely different orders. Why? It almost hurt him to think about it — how could anybody read that and not talk their head off about it? One version, but not both, could be right. One was wrong. And the Bible was supposed to be right all the way through.

And then there was that other thing, where he had stopped reading a few nights earlier. As plain as the nose on your face, in Genesis 6:

> And it came to pass, when men began to multiply on the face of the earth, and daughters were born unto them,
> That the sons of God saw the daughters of men that they were fair; and they took them wives of all which they chose.

He saw these sons of God walking around on earth marrying the daughters of earth men. But Jesus was supposed to have been the only begotten son of God. "Dear God," he prayed again. "Help me to understand thy word. Guide and direct me." These verses were clear. Plain English. Second Timothy 3:16 said, "All scripture is given by inspiration of God."

The next morning Henry and Clearwater sat across from each other, eating breakfast at a table in Mae's Café. Henry told him about the cat. But he kept it short. "My Bible-selling teacher talked to us a lot about selling Bibles, and I had to keep thinking what he said about 'improvise.'" He wanted Mr. Clearwater to bring up the job thing, so he'd keep quiet about all that in Genesis — for the time being, anyway. He dipped the corner of his toast into his mixed-together eggs and grits.

"Okay," said Mr. Clearwater. He wiped his mouth with his napkin. "This job. It's not the kind of business I can tell just anybody about. I work for the FBI." He pulled out his billfold and opened it. A badge. He was a G-man! "We infiltrated a gang of car thieves about six months ago," he said. "They work from here to California, mostly in the southern part of the United States, and then all up and down California. They steal a car — hot-wire it, normally — get it painted unless it's black, an ignition system installed, and then they might sell it, or drive it to California, or turn it over to somebody else, whatever. I get the ones that they're selling, usually. Hadn't had to drive anything to California yet. And what I need is a driver, because that's my Chrysler out there, and sometimes I'm dealing with two cars at a time, and even when I've got just one car, I like to have somebody driving for me."

"So you know J. Edgar Hoover — you're a actual G-man?" This was far better than Henry could have imagined.

"Oh yes. J. Edgar and me are pretty good buddies. I've shot pool with him, eat supper with him, but he don't let nobody know that he shoots pool, see. He's a Christian, like you . . . and me."

"I'll take it. It sounds like a good job." He wished he could tell Uncle Jack. Aunt Dorie would be afraid, though.

Clearwater extended his hand. "Good. We'll start tomorrow. I think we'll have a pickup tomorrow afternoon. Be ready at three o'clock to leave here in the Chrysler and meet me at a place I'll draw out for you on a map. And in a few months from now, when everything is lined up, we'll be making a big number of arrests, all on the same day. All you'll have to do in the meantime is drive for me. You'll make more money than you do selling Bibles, I can tell you that. Twenty-five dollars for every car we move, and that'll be, oh, up to three or four a week."

Henry's mind went: *A hundred dollars in a week.*

"Then some days we just sit," said Clearwater. "It's kind of off and on."

Henry looked around at other people eating breakfast. They were so normal. Nothing like this going on in their lives. They were farmers and regular people. "Can I keep selling Bibles?"

"As long as we're clear about when you go out and when you get back. I need you on call, more or less."

"Am I supposed to dress up like you?"

"Not necessarily. You might get a hat or some hair oil and put the end of your belt where it belongs."

"What's a pickup?"

"I said you might get a hat or some hair oil and use your belt loops."

"Sure. Yes sir."

"A pickup is a car delivery. Somebody will deliver me a car. And another thing: You don't ever, under any circumstances, tell *any*body what you're doing. In fact, you have to take an oath. We'll do it on one of your Bibles before our first gig. If you do tell somebody, it could cause the whole FBI undercover department to fall apart."

"Okay."

"I'll be getting coded messages — general delivery — here and there, and messages at certain motels. This one, for example. I don't actually do the stealing, normally, though I have been asked to do that once or twice. They deliver me a car to drive somewhere, or to get painted, and then we'll do it all over again. You'll be waiting for me somewhere, I get the pickup and drive it to you. All you do is drive. And if you ever by chance get arrested and I'm not around, then all you have to say is 'Code Mercury,' and then your name and my name, Preston Clearwater. No matter what they do or ask you, or how many times, that's all you have to say."

"Do these car thieves ever kill anybody?" asked Henry.

"You don't ever know with these types." Clearwater motioned for the waitress.

"It don't sound too dangerous, though. Just driving."

"It's not at all dangerous. I'll get this breakfast. You can pay your part when we eat from here on out."

Henry was astonished that he could make so much money doing anything, especially while gaining a kind of glory. It sounded like a comic book adventure, or something from the movies. He'd be serving God in a different way. Good against evil. He remembered the pictures in Aunt Dorie's *Children's Book of Bible Stories:* David facing the giant, Goliath, and then the picture of him about to cut Goliath's head off; he saw the picture of Jesus and the money changers — of Jesus chasing them away from the temple. He'd be dealing with bad people. He'd be righting wrong in a way he'd never dreamed of. Parts of the Bible had to do with all this, parts about the Pharisees, and Babylonians, and Roman soldiers, with sin and evil, and good — and all that was true, for sure — and all of that is what he would be a part of, in modern times. He'd probably figure out these Genesis things. He was going to go ahead and read past Genesis 6, anyway, just to see if there were more confusions. This was way back when maybe things got a little mixed up, before people could read and write, when all they could do was tell things.

Clearwater felt like he'd stumbled onto a gift. This boy had some enthusiasm, some energy, and as long as he kept him the right distance from the action — in the dark, that is — he'd be able to work Blinky's route on down into Georgia and Florida, and then back up into the Carolinas, where they could visit some mill bosses, some big tobacco men, relieve them of a few fine cars. He'd gotten a raise on the cars from twenty-five percent to forty percent, and if he didn't get caught or otherwise mess up, then by the time he met with Blinky again, his two-year road quota would be made and he'd be able to move up into more advanced jobs.

That night Henry continued reading in Genesis. About Abraham and Sarah, when their names were Abram and Sarai. He hadn't known about a name change until he jumped ahead and figured it out. But when he jumped ahead he found out about Abraham saying for some reason that his wife Sarah was his sister. He had forgotten that Abraham had a wife, then he remembered: they'd had a baby when they were real old. And he certainly had never heard about what he read in Genesis 16, and then reread.

Now Sarai, Abram's wife, bare him no children: and
she had an handmaid, an Egyptian, whose name was
Hagar.

And Sarai said unto Abram, Behold now, the LORD
hath restrained me from bearing: I pray thee, go in
unto my maid; it may be that I may obtain children by
her. And Abram harkened to the voice of Sarai.

Henry saw that "go in unto" meant go to bed with her
and have a sex relation. It was as plain as day. He kept reading. Abraham *did it*. God wrote it and didn't worry a whiff
about it, not a whiff. *Nobody* was bothered by it.

Something was wrong. The God that wrote this was not
the God he'd been taught to pray to.

Why should he not have a sex relation or two before he
was married? Outside of marriage, like Abraham.

He kept reading, skipping around, past Joseph's coat of
many colors and his brothers and the hidden cup. He'd heard
all that. Then he read in Genesis 38 about a woman named
Tamar, and when he finished that one he had to put down his
Bible and walk outside and look up at the sky and say, "What
in the world?"

So that more or less settled that. He wouldn't have to
wait until he got married. Why shouldn't he do what they
were doing in the very Bible — the good guys, with no consequences? Else the consequences would be mentioned, because God would want them mentioned.

It was three a.m. and he needed to go to sleep. He didn't
know what to pray.

MR. SIM SIMPSON BEATEN, NEW CAR STOLEN

WINSTON-SALEM, N.C. — Clarence "Sim" Simpson reported yesterday that he was assaulted by a stranger and his DeSoto automobile was stolen and driven away, leaving him helpless and injured on the ground in the parking lot behind Clark's Furniture Store just south of town. Simpson was carried by bystanders to Leeds Hospital and released after treatment for a skull fracture.

Mr. Simpson is a retired Army master sergeant and now owns several grocery stores in the area.

Simpson reported that his car was taken in broad daylight by a man with long black hair, wearing a derby hat and sunglasses. The man was alone, seated in Simpson's car, and claimed the car was his when Simpson approached him. Simpson said the man must have hot-wired the DeSoto while Simpson was buying a sofa in Clark's Furniture Store.

"I thought he'd made a normal mistake and got in the wrong car," said the injured Simpson. "And when he picked up a crow bar out of the floor board, I couldn't imagine what it was for. Next thing I knew I was flat on my back."

A witness, Ned Seagroves, reported that the car headed south on County Highway.

PART II

___

GENESIS

1937

___

WHEN HENRY WAS SEVEN

Henry held the army blankets like he might hold a dog — leaning back just a bit so he wouldn't topple forward. Mrs. Albright's faded red plank house, his destination, stood down the hard-frozen dirt road, the morning sun lighting the side of it.

New electric wires, strung from poles, hummed and seemed to silence the rest of the world. Frost sparkled in the road ditch. Henry was glad he wore his hat with the warm, furry earflaps — Aunt Dorie had pulled them down tight over his ears.

He was on a mission for God and Jesus, taking the blankets to Mrs. Albright and her son, Yancy. Trixie followed along behind, stopped, sniffed, squatted to pee near the ditch, steam rising through slanting sunlight. The hair around her mouth was gray.

"That is one odd bird down there," Uncle Jack had said over and over about Yancy, the son. "One odd bird. And all them cats. I bet she's got a sandbox in there as big as a barn door. God a-mighty."

Last night Henry and Uncle Jack played carom, with Uncle Jack leaning over Henry's back, a matchstick in his mouth, showing Henry how to hold the carom stick like a pool cue. Uncle Jack was a little bit hard and cold sometimes, but funny too. Aunt Dorie was warm — and always the same. Uncle Jack forgot he had his matchstick in his mouth and kissed a baby on the head one time and made it cry.

Small, frosty bushes lined the dirt walkway to Mrs. Albright's front door. She wore a black dress and black hat to church every Sunday and sat beside her odd son in a pew halfway down the right side.

Henry opened the screen door and stepped onto the porch — it was dark and quiet in there — and knocked on the front door. It opened and Mrs. Albright smiled at him and bent down. A toothbrush twig stuck out from her mouth, and snuff juice had started little rivers from the corners. "Well, hey there, little Henry."

"I brung you some blankets," said Henry. "May God bless you." Henry smelled snuff and another smell too, coming from inside the house, something that had a little bit of a dirt and stink and fertilizer smell in it.

"God bless *you*, son. Come on in the house and let me give you a little pretty or a piece of candy or something." She took him by the arm. "It's mighty cold out there, ain't it? We can always use blankets." She closed the door behind him. "Always use blankets. Can't have too many."

Several cats came into view and then more — cats that weren't moving much, lolling around, some very still, one licking its shoulder. "It's like a cat heaven and hell down there," Uncle Jack had said. "A hundred cats that talk."

A fire blazed in the fireplace. "We can sure use a couple of blankets," said Mrs. Albright. "Yes sir. We sure can."

Henry wanted to go home. It was dark and hot. Mrs. Albright's and Mrs. Tyler's houses were the only two without electricity. Uncle Jack had said, "She gets electricity down there and one of them cats'll get his tail stuck in a outlet and blow up."

Mrs. Albright held his lapel. "Let me have your coat and hat, son."

Yancy, dressed in blue flannel pajamas, emerged from behind a closed door. The ball on his neck was a "broiter" or something like that.

"We got company, Yancy. Get outen your pajamas."

Yancy threw up a hand and smiled his odd smile. Yancy was a grown man, but he wasn't too tall, and Aunt Dorie said he had the mind of a child. He had a round face that was kind of red, especially around his chin — and the ball down on his neck between his chin and ear was red too. His forehead had a crowd of bumps and wispy hair. He made

sounds. He turned back into his room. He always did what
Mrs. Albright said to do. "At least he's well behaved," people
said. And everybody knew he didn't like the cats.

Mrs. Albright led Henry to a chair in which a calico cat
lay, looking up at them. "Git outen the chair, Angel," said
Mrs. Albright.

Angel had a bobbed tail and only one eye open. Crust
lined the slit of the other.

"Git!" Mrs. Albright waved her arm.

When the cat lit on the floor she turned to look at Henry
over her shoulder and said, in a little high voice, "Glory to
God in the highest! Peace on earth, goodwill toward men!"
then strode away, her shoulders slowly rising one after the
other like she was Miss Smarty-Pants.

Mrs. Albright said to Henry, "You sit down. That one sitting beside the wood is Moses. Have you ever seen any other
cats that can talk, Henry-Boy?"

"No ma'am."

"Say something, Moses."

"I was found in the bulrushes," he squeaked. "I said to
the pharaoh: 'Let my people go!'"

It was Mrs. Albright talking. That's what it was. She was
throwing her voice. He wanted to get on back home, maybe.
Unless she had that little pretty, or a piece of candy.

"Don't you tell nobody my cats talk, now, you hear? Especially no little children."

"Yes ma'am."

"Now, would you like some corn bread and molasses or a
piece of candy?"

"A piece of candy."

"Good. I ain't got no corn bread, anyway." She laughed. "You're all boy, ain't you? All boy." She moved into the kitchen. "Judas. Git off the table."

Judas said, "I'm gonna hang myself by the neck, I messed up so bad, or cut open my stomach."

"Git off there."

Henry heard the soft thump of cat feet hitting the floor.

Judas said, "If I had a gun, I'd shoot myself."

Yancy, dressed in overalls and long johns, came out again, moved a cat away from his doorway with his foot, closed the door.

"Here you go," said Mrs. Albright. "A stick of red-and-white candy. Your Aunt Dorie is the best thing." She looked at Yancy. "She sent us some blankets, Yancy." She bent closer to Henry. "*BOO!* Ah-ha-ha-ha-ha. Did I scare you?"

"Yes ma'am."

"Yancy, bring me that pad and pencil.

"Let's see now. Let me write a nice note here. A nice note. 'Thank you God for Christian neighbors' is a note I could write to God, now, couldn't I, Henry?"

"Yes ma'am."

Mrs. Albright held her hand to Henry's shoulder as he left through the front door, then she stood on the porch as Henry walked away.

Back inside she went to the kitchen and from a whiskey bottle poured a little of her gold liquid into a glass, added some water, walked back to the living room, and sat in her favorite chair.

Isaac said to Paul, "He's the one his daddy got killed by the truck timber, ain't he?"

"That's right," said Paul. "When he was a baby."

"He might consider himself lucky," said Isaac, "that he didn't have no stinky old man to give him grief on the mountain."

"There're more mountains than one, you know." Paul rolled onto his back, curled his paws in, closed his eyes.

"You traveled around too much," said Isaac, "entirely too much. You should have stayed home more, raised a family."

Angel and Mary Magdalene stood, stretched, and moved toward the kitchen.

Judas jumped into Mrs. Albright's lap and purred.

Mrs. Albright took a little sip of the devil's disciple, placed her hand on Judas's neck, looked down at him.

Back in his yard, Henry didn't notice the shiny black car in the driveway until he almost walked into it.

Inside, Aunt Dorie sat on the living room couch, and on the floor nearby a man knelt beside an open valise and several Bibles. He was dressed like a gentleman and had silver hair. He looked up and said, "This must be the young man."

Aunt Dorie had taken off her apron, Henry saw, but still had the green scarf on her head. "Henry, this is a Bible salesman, Mr. . . . I'm sorry I —"

"Levingson, Mr. Levingson." Still kneeling, he extended

his hand to Henry, looked back at Aunt Dorie. "Just call me Tommy."

Henry almost stopped and stepped backward, but he didn't. He took the hand.

"What a handsome young man," said Mr. Levingson. "You were certainly right about that. Your mama told me all about you, son. She tells me you've started memorizing scripture."

"I'm his aunt," said Aunt Dorie.

"Your aunt, I mean."

Aunt Dorie said, "Recite John three, sixteen, and Timothy three, sixteen, son."

"John three, sixteen," said Henry. "'For God so loved the world, that he gave his only begotten Son, that whosoever believeth in him should not perish, but have everlasting life.' Timothy three, sixteen: 'All scripture is given by inspiration of God, and is profitable for doctrine, for reproof, for correction, for instruction in righteousness.'"

"Goodness gracious," said Mr. Levingson. He could smell that they'd had bacon for breakfast, and he hoped the lady might offer him a little something to eat. "She told me you were going to grow up to be a Christian gentleman. And I'll bet you will."

"He's won the Bible sword drill in his age group twice this year already," said Aunt Dorie, her eyes still on Henry.

"Sword drill?"

"You never did sword drills?"

"No ma'am. I was a, ah, Presby — *am* a Presbyterian."

"Well, have you got a Bible Henry can hold? And one you can hold? We'll show you."

"Here you go." Mr. Levingson handed Henry a Bible and got one for himself out of his valise. What the hell is this? he was thinking.

"Okay, now," said Aunt Dorie, "you-all stand side by side and pretend there were six or eight more children standing beside you. I'll just move to this chair so you can face me. I'm the general. Okay, now. Hold the Bible down by your side," she said to Levingson. "You watch Henry and you'll see how it works."

Levingson glanced down at the boy, held the Bible at his side in his right hand. He sure hadn't counted on something like this.

Aunt Dorie said, "Atten*tion*."

The boy jerked to attention. Levingson did too.

"Draw *swords*."

What the —? The boy snapped his Bible to a position in front of him, held the Bible as if he were about to open it — left hand on top, right on bottom. Levingson did the same. Wait a minute, he wasn't going to have to . . . She was going to call out a *verse*? And he didn't know from holy crap where anything in there was, except Genesis.

"Prepare to advance," said the woman. "Psalms one hundred, verse five. Charge!"

The boy snapped open his Bible, turned a couple of pages, placed a finger on a page, stepped forward, clicked his heels together.

Holy Christmas! Levingson opened his Bible and pretended to look.

"Henry," said the woman.

"Psalms one hundred, verse five. 'For the Lord is good; his mercy is everlasting, and his truth endureth to all generations.' Psalms one hundred, verse five."

"Very good," said Aunt Dorie. "You beat the Bible salesman. You see how it works?" she said to Mr. Levingson.

"Yes ma'am, I do."

Henry looked at the Bible in Levingson's hands. "Why are you looking in the front?"

"Oh, just kind of . . . messing around. Letting you win."

"You open to the *middle* to get to Psalms. Didn't you know that?"

"Oh yeah. I just —"

"Want to play again?"

"Oh no. I see what a sword drill is now, and I've got to be getting on down the road right soon here."

"Henry, son," said Aunt Dorie, "I reckon it's time you had your own Bible." She reached to the table beside her chair. "I think you ought to have this one. It has India paper and a zipper. Look. Here you go."

The Bible felt thin and a little bit limp. It seemed kind of precious.

Aunt Dorie was proud. Henry was admiring his own Bible, the nice man was standing there, sunlight was coming through the window.

"That's a fine Bible," the man said to Henry. "One of our

best-selling models. We can't keep them in stock. And then the Family Edition," he said to Aunt Dorie, "would be good for the whole family. It's a model that —"

"Henry," said Aunt Dorie, "go get me the scissors off the table in the kitchen."

Henry left, and Dorie said to the Bible salesman, "I'm sorry, we can't afford another Bible. My husband's checking some rabbit boxes, and I just realized he's due back, and he shouldn't know right yet that I'm buying one for Henry even. It's part cigar money I'm using."

"Oh, yes, Mrs. Sorrell. Of course. Let me just get these things together. And I appreciate those names you gave me. May God bless you and all the people you love." He stood, stuck out his hand, bowed a little bow, sort of a neck stretch.

Henry was back with the scissors.

"You be good, son," said the man. "Take care of that Bible. It's a fine one."

As soon as the door closed, Aunt Dorie said, "Look at those pages." She reached over and thumbed a page. "It's India paper, and you can almost see through it."

This Bible felt almost as thin as a New Testament. It was like a little fire truck — not a big clumsy fire truck. It was small and swift and would maybe be easy to understand because it was thin, and it felt good in his hands. "Was he a preacher?" asked Henry.

"He was a Bible salesman. Spreading the Gospel *that* way."

"Why did you need the scissors?"

"Oh, I just need to cut something in a minute."

Henry walked to the front window, saw the man open his car door and place his valise inside, then look over the top of his car down toward Mrs. Albright's house, knock a cigarette up out of a pack, pick it out with his lips, put the pack away, and then light the cigarette with a match cupped in his hands. He looked back at Aunt Dorie's front door before he got in the car. He seemed sad.

He backed out of the driveway, turned, and headed down the hill. He slowed and turned into Mrs. Albright's driveway. Henry wondered about Mrs. Albright's husband. He got killed in a war about the Spanish something. He was a hero and left behind a widow and two children. Uncle Jack said Mrs. Albright's daughter was unhappy because she didn't have anything wrong with her, so she left home. Aunt Dorie said you were supposed to take care of orphans and widows. Widows were not the same as black widows. Black widows ate their husbands, Uncle Jack said.

Dorie walked to the window, stood beside Henry, and looked down toward Mrs. Albright's. "We don't want to worry Uncle Jack about buying a new Bible, so don't say anything to him about it. I'll tell him."

"Since Mrs. Albright had Yancy, does she still have him?" asked Henry.

"She had Yancy, yes," said Aunt Dorie. "What do you mean?"

"Does she have *him* the same way he has that *ball* in his neck?"

"What do you mean?"

"Like you can't throw it away."

"Well, that's right. I guess that's the way it is," said Aunt Dorie.

"But some things you have you *can* throw away."

"That's right."

"Why do they both have the same word, 'have'?"

"I never thought about it. Come on over here and let's look at your Bible."

1939

_____

The teacher, Mr. Harris, talked along. New Sunday school year at Antioch Baptist Church. Henry and five other nine-year-old boys sat in wicker-bottom chairs in the church basement classroom, a framed picture of the twelve-year-old Jesus on the wall — the picture that was on their Sunday school quarterly cover and on the walls in several other rooms throughout the children's classrooms — along with other pictures, including Jesus with little children at his feet, outdoors somewhere.

"God created the light before he created anything else," said Mr. Harris, "and then he made the land and the water and he made it separate. And then he made all the plants.

Then God made the sun and the moon and then after that the stars."

Mr. Harris, a heavyset man wearing a white shirt, one collar point turned upward, and a blue tie with red fishing reels on it that his wife had ordered from a catalog, half sat on and half leaned against a small table in the room. He paused between sentences and looked from one boy to the next. If you kept your eye right on them, one after the other, they were more apt to behave. Teaching these boys was a mission that fed into his view of himself — himself as one of the people that if allowed to run the world could help make it, by golly, a pretty good place. He had a sense of mission. "Then he made the fish and birds," he said. "And then he made all the other animals. Then God made man and woman to have dominion over all the animals."

Mr. Harris owned his own upholstering company now, got all his business learning without any college, and would for sure continue upward in the world when he opened his second store, in Grove Hill. The business world was about fully recovered from the Depression, electricity had arrived, telephones would soon be in every home. He knew that the heathen on other continents would likely come to God, but perhaps not in his lifetime. Revelation 20 said there would be one thousand years of peace under Jesus' rule, and there was too much heathenism going on for it to happen any day soon. Somebody would have to get roads and telephones into all the jungles and mountain areas in the world before that could happen. He himself couldn't travel to Africa because of his business and family, but he could help raise brave and honest young Christian gentlemen who might. "Can somebody tell me," he said, "what 'dominion' means?"

Nobody answered.

"It means man rules over them, over the animals. Does anybody have a pet?"

Floyd Hall raised his hand. "I do."

"Thank goodness somebody can answer a question. What kind of pet, Floyd?"

"A dog." Floyd's paunch had worked his white shirt out on one side, and his hair had grease only in front.

"So who tells your dog what to do?"

"His name is Scout."

Mr. Harris raised his eyebrows. "Who tells him what to do?"

"My daddy."

"That's right. And your daddy is a man, and God made man to have rulership over all the animals. That's why we can go to Africa and shoot lions and tigers."

"My uncle shot a cat," said Henry.

"Yes, and cats too," said Mr. Harris.

"But if a man was in the jungle," said Nicky Noland, "and he didn't have no gun or anything, then a lion could gulp his fat ass right down." He laughed and looked around, several boys smiled a little, one laughed, Henry was startled, and then they all, except for Nicky, turned to look at Mr. Harris. Nicky was still looking at the other boys.

Mr. Harris stood from the table, stepped back, reddened,

and frowned. "You may sit in the chair just outside the door, young man. We don't use that kind of language in this room — or any room in this building."

Nicky caught on. His eyebrows raised and the corners of his mouth dropped, but he didn't speak.

Aunt Dorie had told Henry to stay away from Nicky Noland and his brothers. Somebody brought them to church on the two Sundays of the annual attendance contests with Zion Baptist.

"I'm going home, mister," said Nicky. "I ain't sitting in nobody's fat-ass chair. I never wanted to come in here in the first place." The door slammed behind him.

"Well, that is one way, boys, you do not want to be." Mr. Harris paced. "You do not want to be disobedient and ugly. Now, listen to me." Mr. Harris was upset, and thus he had the full attention of the boys. "God made man smart enough to make a gun that can kill a lion," he said, "but lions can't make guns to kill men. So you see that God made men smarter than lions or any other animals. That is as clear as the nose on your face." He walked to the door, opened it, looked out, and then came back to his table, where he half sat again. He loosened the top button to his collar. The collar point dropped some. "After God made man and woman he saw that everything was very good. That was the evening of the sixth day when he finished all this, and then on the seventh day he rested because he was tired, and so this day became a very special day. It became the Sabbath, or Sunday, the day we go to church on, and worship and rest."

Henry pictured God being tired. And then, as if it were a big black tadpole swimming up from the depths of a mudhole, a question surfaced. He raised his hand.

"Yes, Henry. Good."

"How could somebody who is perfect get tired?"

"Oh. Well, Henry." Mr. Harris smiled. "That seems like a good question . . . at first, but let's think about it for just a minute." He frowned. "We have to be very careful about what we ask questions about. Because we can commit blasphemy, and blasphemy is a sin. That's just the way it is." Mr. Harris stood up from the little table again. "We don't want to get into any blasphemy, because Jesus will be unhappy with that, now won't he?" He tried to smile.

Henry couldn't think of anything to say. He didn't want to blasphemy. It sounded like a very bad thing. Mr. Harris was a Sunday school teacher, a man who had to know everything about the Bible and God to get his job. No way around that.

"He said what?" asked Uncle Jack.

"That it was blasamy to ask questions about God," said Henry.

"*Blasphemy,*" said Uncle Jack. He sat on the back door steps, leaning back with his legs spread, cleaning a fingernail with the short blade from his four-blade Case. He had bags under his eyes and combed his hair straight back. "Blasphemy." He was chewing a plug, tossing it around fast in his mouth.

Henry sat beside him. It had rained and then cleared up,

and now the late afternoon sky dropped down a soft orange light that seemed to color the air in some strange way, to give green bushes and shrubs a dusty orange glow not theirs.

"Course that don't surprise me," said Uncle Jack. "Bill Harris. Blasphemy, hell."

Henry looked up at his uncle. "He sent Nicky Noland out because he said a bad word."

"What'd he say?"

"Ass."

"Did he tell Harris to kiss his ass?"

"No sir. Nicky said a lion could gulp down a man's . . . a man's . . ."

"A man's ass." Uncle Jack laughed. "Well, he can, can't he?"

"Yessir, but if you say that in church then you might do blasamy and go to hell."

"*Blasphemy*. You got to learn to talk, boy. Tell you what: I'll go with you and Aunt Dorie next Sunday and we'll have a talk with Mr. Bill *Ass* Harris."

"No, Jack," said Aunt Dorie. She'd come out quietly onto the porch and stood behind them. "Bill Harris does a lot for the church, and he's in there on Sunday mornings with them boys when he could be at home sleeping like some people I won't name."

Jack slowly stood. He folded in the blade against his overalls, turned. Henry stayed seated, looking up at him. "Well, Dorie," said Uncle Jack, "Bill Harris is also a . . . a dull man. Them boys would get along just as fine by theirselves."

"I don't think so. Boys need Sunday school."

"Like a . . . like a dog needs a spoon."

Aunt Dorie and Henry sat on the living room couch just before bedtime. Aunt Dorie told him that Mr. Harris and Preacher Gibson both had told Aunt Dorie that Henry was a very smart young man, and that the most important thing for him to know and understand was that Jesus died for him on the cross, for everybody, and that if Henry couldn't understand something, that was okay. All he had to do was believe. She asked him if he believed in Jesus. He said yes. Did he believe in God and the Bible? Yes. She told him as long as he believed in those things, then he was a Christian and he would go to heaven. Once saved, always saved, she said. All he had to do was go down front at church and accept Jesus — when he felt Jesus calling. Because it had to be done publicly.

Henry thought again about God resting on the seventh day. "But why would somebody who's perfect need to rest? Can I ask that if I'm not in church?"

"Yes, you can ask. For a little while sometimes God could be like a man and need some rest, but that don't mean God wasn't perfect. He could do whatever he wanted to. He just probably *wanted* to want to rest. He could be like a man and not like a man when he was inside Jesus because Jesus was God too. *And* Jesus was a man. God the Father is God, Jesus the Son is God, and the Holy Spirit is God. Jesus is perfect even though he cursed the fig tree and even though he cursed the men in the temple who were changing money."

"Why was it okay for Jesus to cuss?"

"Because he was Jesus, and the fig tree and the money changers were bad."

"Could I cuss a fig tree and money changers?"

"Well, no, because you're not Jesus, son."

Henry knew Aunt Dorie was right about the Bible. The Bible was perfect, and it had the Twenty-third Psalm:

The LORD is my shepherd; I shall not want.
He maketh me to lie down in green pastures: he leadeth
     me beside the still waters.
He restoreth my soul: he leadeth me in the paths of
     righteousness for his name's sake.
Yea, though I walk through the valley of the shadow of
     death, I will fear no evil: for thou art with me;
     thy rod and thy staff they comfort me.
Thou preparest a table before me in the presence of
     mine enemies: thou anointest my head with oil;
     my cup runneth over.
Surely goodness and mercy shall follow me all the days
     of my life: and I will dwell in the house of the
     LORD for ever.

Besides hearing Pa Dampier read the Twenty-third Psalm at the family reunion each year, Henry heard it, as a prayer, from Aunt Dorie and in church — read by Preacher Gibson or somebody else. And it had somehow *gained a life.* When Henry heard it or read it, he saw a shepherd with a staff, like the picture of Jesus in *The Children's Book of Bible Stories,* and the picture of David with his staff in there too. He saw the green pastures, the same as on the mural on the wall behind the baptism place up front in the church. Yes, the Twenty-third Psalm had its own life, like some hymns were starting to have for him. "Love Lifted Me" showed a man sinking into the ocean with his hand up. "The Old Rugged Cross" showed a cross on a hill with rags hanging and a bunch of women kneeling around it, crying. "What a Friend We Have in Jesus" showed Jesus and Henry walking down a dirt road together. "Just As I Am" showed Mrs. Albright's Yancy walking down the aisle on the right-hand side of the church, crying, and then leaning into the arms of Preacher Gibson. "Bringing in the Sheaves" showed these big groups of people walking across Egypt, bringing in things.

In the Twenty-third Psalm, the still waters were the pond at Pa D's farm and scared Henry just a little. But nothing came to him for "restoreth my soul" and "the paths of righteousness," though he figured it might have something to do with a path around the pond. And then the big, harsh idea of the dark valley of the shadow of death, where vines grew along craggy hillsides with the tree branches that caught that man by his hair — the man with a hard name who was David's son — and who later got his head cut off and made David sad. There was no need for Henry to fear, because the Lord was Jesus, and with his rod and staff he would save

Henry from anything bad. "Thy rod and thy staff they comfort me," comfort meaning being in bed with Aunt Dorie and
her soft pillow and her reading from *The Children's Book of
Bible Stories,* though Henry never quite knew the difference
between a rod and a staff — there was that "spare the rod and
spoil the child" that people talked about, except Uncle Jack
used a switch, one that Henry had to choose off the bushes
in the backyard, so maybe a rod was just a straight stick.
What Henry saw in Jesus' hand was the long stick with the
curved end for the sheeps' necks, and then maybe a stick of
some sort, a rod, was on the ground — "thy rod and thy staff
they comfort me." Jesus did get mad: at the fig tree and at the
money changers. Then next came "Thou preparest a table
before me in the presence of mine enemies." Enemies were
Indians or Philistines or something like that. Jesus said for-
give your enemies, but God killed a lot of them — especially
when the Red Sea parted and then came back in on top of all
those Egyptians. But Jesus didn't kill anybody. He loved his
enemies. And then that about oil on his head. He saw oil on
a man's forehead, curly hair, and the oil shiny, and he clearly
saw the cup runneth over — it was Uncle Jack's coffee cup —
over into the saucer and then onto the tablecloth, with Aunt
Dorie standing there looking on; and then, finally, there
would be good things all his life, and he would "dwell in the
house of the Lord for ever" — because he believed in God.

He memorized the Twenty-third Psalm for his Sunday
school class and drew a picture of the road that went on forever, on past the end of this life and into his life in heaven.

1930

WHEN HENRY WAS A BABY

WESTERN UNION

received at 99 CF COLLECT
Simmons NCAR 755P May 3 1930
Mr. and Mrs. Samuel Cleary
Rt 6 GARDEN SPR FLA

DANNY HIT BY PIECE OF WOOD FROM TRUCK
IN HOSPITAL MORE SOON

DORIE

819P

WESTERN UNION

received at 233 CF COLLECT
Simmons NCAR 544P May 4 1930
Mr. and Mrs. Samuel Cleary
Rt 6 GARDEN SPR FLA

DANNY DIED UNEXPECTED FROM ACCIDENT
FUNERAL ON WED AT 3 PM PLEASE COME ON

DORIE

630P

Caroline's school desk had a *T* carved in it, and she traced it with her finger. She was in the first grade. Her father had been dead for a week now, and the man in the truck who caused him to die might go to prison for it, and sometimes she dreamed it was all pretend. In the dream, she'd go to a room where her daddy might be, but when she got there the roof of the room would be gone, leaving a blue sky and moving white clouds above, and nobody would be in the room. Her daddy had gone up to heaven. He got hit by the plank sticking out from the truck and died.

Back at home, Henry, the baby, lay on a quilt on the kitchen floor.

The dog had got in the diaper pail and dragged diapers through the pushed-out screen and into the yard.

Libby, Henry's mother, saw the diapers when she came into the yard from milking. She hadn't been able to fix the screen that the dog had pushed out.

She would have to sell the goddamned cow. She'd rather be dead than this. She'd rather be in some kind of pain in a hospital where nurses could bring food and water and medicine, and wash her sheets and pajamas. Danny would've fixed the screen as soon as that happened, and he'd have whipped the dog for pushing it out.

She got the loaded shotgun and an extra shell. Called the dog. She'd have to get a ways away from the house, because she didn't have the energy to dig a grave. So she kept walking — the dog following — on by the dried-up cornstalks from the year before and finally stopped atop the bank that led down to the creek, and that's where she stood, pulling back the stiff hammers, remembering her daddy, standing out in the field of stubble tobacco stalks that time as he raised the shotgun, his shoulder being kicked back, the top of a stray dog's head lifting off like a little wig in the wind. The dog had killed a chicken.

Libby shot the dog twice, reloaded, and shot him again, walked back to the cabin, put the shotgun back, and picked up the crying baby, laid him on the water shelf on the porch, and took off the diaper — he had a bad rash — and cleaned him up. And then back inside she put a clean diaper on him — well, it was dry anyway — then a small clean flour sack with holes for head and arms, and then wrapped him in a quarter sheet and put a blanket in a cardboard kindling box and put him in that. She went to the sewing machine and got the money in the brown envelope. She stood for a second and looked at the sewing machine. Dorie would want it and would get it. Libby had never got the hang of figuring out a pattern, of the pumping with her foot, the threading and holding and stretching and going slow and going fast. Dorie had tried to teach her. She liked Dorie, because Dorie had given her the time of day.

She got an armful of clothes and stuffed them into a paper sack along with shoes, razor and blades, toothbrush, hairbrush, and mirror. On the way to the truck she got a whiff of breeze from the hog lot.

She put the baby on the truck seat beside her and her things. He'd stopped crying. She wouldn't look at him.

She drove to Pa D's and stopped the car and got out. She felt hot around her ears and down her neck. Ma D and Pa D and the rest were in the fields or barns. She was glad somebody hadn't come to sit on the porch. She took the box from the front seat and, not looking down into it, took it inside and left it on the kitchen table with a note saying that Caroline would be coming home on the school bus. She did not look around.

She would not think the child's name.

The air around her on the porch seemed cool and a thousand miles away, even though it was right there against her arms. She stood with her head dropped low and watched tears hit the floor planks as her shoulders shook, watched drip from her nose lengthen down in a string. She held her hands, clutched, at her sides. Henry. Caroline. Danny. She went back in and wrote a note to Caroline, saying good-bye, saying that Caroline would be happier now — that everybody would be happier now, and that she was sorry.

Rather than turn left and drive back home, she turned right and headed toward Raleigh. She had more than forty dollars.

At Sunday dinner at the homeplace, Pa D, after reaching for a biscuit, told everybody that somebody ought to go ahead and decide for sure who got the two children and make it official. Pa D wore suspenders and had a watermelon belly that kind of ran out onto his legs as he sat.

Jack and Dorie, sitting for a few minutes on their front porch after driving home, talked.

Dorie said, "It's hard to think about them separated up. She's a sweet girl and could help take care of him."

"I know she's a sweet girl. But we got to make a decision. Ruth is begging for her, and that'll work out good. Her war pension will go up, and she can move next door easy enough."

As usual, some came to Pa and Ma D's for the family reunion early on the Saturday of Memorial Day weekend and spent the night. Others came for Sunday dinner only; some stayed after Sunday dinner for horseshoes and swimming. Most adults who stayed overnight played Rook on Saturday night.

Uncle Delbert's wife, Sis, after both families gathered in the house for Sunday dinner at one-thirty, clanked a glass with a fork. "Okay, everybody, listen up. Before Pa D says the blessing, Caroline is going to say Grandma Caroline's name. Caroline, come here, honey."

Caroline came to the sink and Aunt Sis picked her up and stood her in a chair.

"Speak it out, now, honey," said Aunt Sis.

Caroline looked at all the faces, then at Aunt Sis, and holding her eyes there, spoke: "Cora Rosa Hunter Novella Caroline Hildred Martha Bird Taylor Copeland."

Scattered applause.

"Now, what did Grandpa Walker call her?"

"Puss."

Laughs.

"Pa D will return thanks," said Aunt Sis. "Pa D?"

"Who let that dog in?" somebody asked.

"He just come in."

"Well, run him out."

Pa D made his way forward, thumbed open his Bible, and read the Twenty-third Psalm, what he always read, ending:

. . . and I will dwell in the house of the LORD for ever.

Then, "Let us pray. Dear Lord, make us thankful for these and the many blessings thou hast given us, and be with the soul of departed Danny. In thy blessed name, amen."

People gathered in the kitchen to serve plates for children

and for themselves — fried chicken, beans, peas, beef, ham, creamed potatoes, deviled eggs, pickles, biscuits, corn bread, relish, corn, potato salad — hot and cold and warm foods together, smelling sweet along with the already-there smells of Pa D and Ma D's house, and the sounds of voices and dogs outside, and the Twenty-third Psalm, all melding into an almost singular sensation that these people would be reminded of once or twice a year in some place they didn't expect it.

Two women met in a bedroom and nursed their babies. One, feeling uneasy in a way she couldn't quite understand, told her cousin that Uncle Brother had just said that the only difference between a woman having a baby and a pig having a baby was that the woman squealed louder. That was just like Uncle Brother, always joshing, but the comparison brought an uneasiness that she understood only enough to laugh away.

At a card table on the porch, Jack sat with his brother-in-law Delbert and brother-in-law Samuel, and a new in-law, Manley, freshly married to Dorcus, Delbert and Sis's daughter. Not being able to remember all the names was a problem for most of the adults, except for Sis. People who needed a name went to Aunt Sis.

Samuel and Linda and their three children — Carson was the youngest — had driven up from Garden Springs, Florida, where they worked for a rich man, running one of his orange groves. But Linda was asleep in the back bedroom. She was Dorie's sister. She often looked weak and pale, especially after the long auto journey up from Florida. Samuel had said the illness was God's will. He spoke of Job.

Jack normally did not sit with Samuel for the meal, because of grudges, some forgotten, but today Jack had missed the biscuits somehow, and while he was gone back to the kitchen for a couple of minutes, Samuel sat down at the card table across from Jack's seat.

When Jack came back, Samuel kept his seat anyway.

"Do you go to church?" Jack, chewing a bite of biscuit, asked Manley, the newlywed.

"I go with Dorcus, yeah. I'll be going with her."

"Well, did I ever tell you about my dog's Bible?"

"No sir."

Samuel stood. "I've heard all this before." He placed his silverware on his plate, looked around for a seat, picked up his glass of tea.

"Aw, sit down, Sam," said Jack.

"Samuel," said Samuel.

"Sit down," said Delbert.

"Samuel," said Jack. "Excuse me. Sit down. Get the corncob out your ass." Then he said to a boy at the next table, "Could you pass me that chicken one more time? I meant to get a wing. And you-all eat some of that rabbit stew in there on the stove. I made it."

"I just don't care to hear about Trixie's Bible again," said Samuel. "No thank you." He moved away.

Jack looked at Samuel's back, then turned to Manley. "Trixie, my dog, has got this Bible. It's got two verses. One: 'There ain't no magic and never was.' Number two: 'Nobody can see into the future.' A dog wrote it over five thousand years ago, and it cuts through a lot of" — he whispered — "shit." He took a swig of ice tea. "How do you like it so far?" he asked Manley.

"What — married life?"

"No. The family."

"It's all right. It's good. I think it's good you-all took in the boy. And Aunt Ruth, the girl."

That afternoon Uncle Jack, Aunt Dorie, Caroline, the baby Henry, and Trixie got to the pond first — for swimming. A pasture lay between the house and the pond. At one end of the pond was the dam with a diving board, and at the other, a grassy bank where people rested on towels and in lawn chairs near the main wading place. Pine trees bordered the back side of the pond.

Caroline sat on the grass on a white towel and watched Uncle Jack stand at the edge of the pond in his swimsuit and unbuttoned shirt and shoes without socks. He chewed a plug of tobacco. He pulled a cigarillo from his shirt pocket — the shirttail out. He looked at it, put it in his mouth, lit it, and then went back to chewing — not like an average man would chew tobacco, but nervously, rapidly. Caroline had seen him stand like this at the pond every year after the reunion dinner, while everybody waited for an hour after eating so they wouldn't have a stomach cramp and drown. Her daddy would do the same thing back before he got hit by the piece of timber — he would stand there with Uncle Jack. But he didn't chew. And he wouldn't go into the water. He'd just talk to Uncle Jack while they stood there, and then Uncle Jack, after the hour was up, would walk slowly into the water. Sometimes Caroline's mother had been sick and hadn't been able to come to the family reunion. But her daddy always did.

Aunt Dorie sat on a towel with the baby, Henry.

The cigarillo hung in Uncle Jack's mouth, with him taking puffs and chewing at the same time, and then he kicked his shoes off, took off his shirt, dropped it, and walked into the water.

On the ground beside Caroline was an inner tube inside sewn-together tow sacks — a raft for floating on.

Trixie ambled over, her tail wagging.

Aunt Dorie put the baby in her lap and rubbed his back, while Uncle Jack waded into deeper and deeper water, until he was in almost up to his shoulders. The cigarillo still dangled, untouched, and he puffed on it while tossing the chew tobacco around in his mouth. He crossed his arms and stood there like that. Way out there. And then Aunt Dorie picked up Henry and pulled the float into the water a little ways and plopped Henry down on it and floated him in a circle. Way down at the end of the pond a boy dove off the diving board. Another boy followed. They were yelling and laughing.

Caroline stood and stepped into the pond, walked out, looking down into the murky water lit by streaks of sun rays, water up to her knees and then up to her waist. It was cool water with cold spots here and there at her ankles and feet. Her daddy had taught her to swim the summer before. He said everybody had to learn when they were six. Now he wasn't in the world to teach Henry. She wondered if he might come walking up out of the woods and say he'd just had to go away for a while. She wondered where her mother was. But she didn't mind living with Aunt Ruth. Her mama had scared her a lot sometimes by staring out the window while Caroline talked to her.

She fell onto her back and floated, kicking her feet — the part about swimming she'd learned first. The back of her head was almost cold, after getting hot in the sun.

When she came back onto shore, Aunt Dorie told her to sit with Henry while she swam out to Uncle Jack. Once Aunt Dorie got way out there, and Uncle Jack started horsing around with her, Caroline decided she'd take Henry for a little ride on the inner tube. That new man who'd married Dorcus was rowing Dorcus in a boat.

Caroline managed to get Henry on the inner tube and then float it in very shallow water at the edge of the pond, and then on a little deeper. She watched Henry look at the water, waited for him to start crying, but he didn't. He seemed pleased, and so she walked him into waist-deep water. Dorcus and her new husband rowed their boat right up to Uncle Jack and Aunt Dorie.

Caroline looked back to the inner tube. It was empty. She looked first on shore, then at the long, wide surface of the pond — as smooth and calm as it could be — and she started to scream but swallowed it and dove beneath the tube with both eyes wide open, a deep orange muddy color in front of her. She grasped forward with her hands. Her right hand was suddenly touching — and then her fingers were around — Henry's thigh. She found one ankle and then the other and lifted as she stood straight.

She heard Aunt Dorie shout, "Caroline, what are you doing?" She looked out where Aunt Dorie and Uncle Jack stood. "Nothing," she shouted. "Teaching him to swim."

"Put him back up on the beach, sweetie."

"Okay."

She held him a foot or so above the water like he was lying on his stomach, his nose down, and shook him. He coughed, struggled, and then threw up water, milk, and other stuff, something yellow, as she waded with him toward the shore.

Uncle Jack hollered, "Don't let that float float off!"

A sob pushed out from her. She sat down on the white towel, holding Henry, looking out to Aunt Dorie and Uncle Jack and then down at her brother. He was more precious than the world. And now she had a big secret, unless Dorcus or her new husband had seen . . . But here came Aunt Linda holding her baby, Carson, in her arms. She was talking to him. She hadn't noticed. Henry looked okay, except he was a little blue maybe. He held up his hand and looked at it as if he'd never seen it before. Aunt Linda walked up and set baby Carson beside Henry. "Well, what's been going on?" she said.

"I been teaching him to swim. Pretend. He got some water in his mouth."

"It'll be fun when him and Carson get old enough to play together."

"Yes ma'am."

Later Caroline begged Aunt Ruth to let her spend that night with Henry. She sort of wanted to keep an eye on him. Drowning might could go ahead and happen anyway — a few hours after somebody got saved. Aunt Ruth said fine, as long as it was all right with Aunt Dorie. And it was.

After her bedtime, Caroline, almost asleep, lay on the cot against the bedroom wall, still afraid for Henry, listening for talk and movement.

"Let's get you a fresh diaper," said Aunt Dorie to Henry.

"Look," said Uncle Jack. "He's got a woody."

"Jack. You shouldn't be talking that way. Caroline might be awake."

"She's asleep. He'd rather play with that thing than win money."

"Jack! Be quiet."

Caroline wondered if a woody was something caused by Henry almost drowning. What was he playing with? She saw a small piece of wood stuck to his side somehow. She thought about the big plank that killed her daddy, and the man who drove the truck.

1933

———

Henry, in Aunt Dorie's lap, wore the blue pajamas that Santa Claus had brought him. Aunt Dorie sat up in bed. He listened as she finished the story of Joseph and his coat of many colors from *The Children's Book of Bible Stories*, and then as she read aloud to him from a thin, blue book: "All the king's horses and all the king's men couldn't put Humpty Dumpty together again."

Jack, propped up on the other side of the bed, read the newspaper, folded so he could hold it in one hand. A cigarillo and a kitchen match hung between his lips.

"Why couldn't they put him together?" Henry asked Dorie.

"He was broke."

"Why was he bloke?"

"He fell off a wall."

"Why?"

"He just did."

"Why?"

"I don't know. It doesn't say, sweetie."

"Read it again."

Dorie read the nursery rhyme.

"Who was the king?"

"He was the head man in England."

"Did he know Moses?"

"I don't think he did."

"Did God know the king?"

"I guess he did. Yes, he did. God knows everybody."

"Did Jesus know the king?"

"I don't know. I don't think so. He was at a different time."

Later, after Henry was asleep on his thick pallet, Jack looked over. "I just think you should read him nursery rhymes and comic books. That Bible-story book . . ."

"What?"

"Where's it at?"

"What?"

"That book of Bible stories."

"Right here on the table."

"Hand it here. Which one were you on?"

"Joseph. It's from the Bible, Jack. Let's don't do this again now," said Dorie.

"I'll just open it. Okay. So here we go. Adam and Eve. Poor them."

"Let's don't do this in front of Henry."

"He's asleep."

"You read to him if you don't like what I read."

"I'll tell him some stories. And you show me a man that won't eat a apple hanging in his own yard and I'll show you a . . . wimpy man."

The next night, in bed, Dorie rested her head back with her eyes closed. Henry sat in Uncle Jack's lap, facing him.

"Now," said Uncle Jack. "Once upon a time there was this old woman lived way out in the woods by herself, and every night she cooked biscuits and gravy for supper, and while she was cooking she'd go to the door and say, 'Who's a-coming to eat biscuits and gravy with me tonight?' And nobody ever answered, except one night this voice from way off says, 'I'm a-coming.' So she went back inside and started fixing biscuits and gravy, then in a little bit went back to the door and said, 'Who's a-coming to eat biscuits and gravy with me tonight?' And not that far off a voice says, 'I'm a-coming.' So she went back in and finished up with the biscuits and gravy and then came back to the door and said, 'Who's a-coming to eat biscuits and gravy with me tonight?' and right around the corner of the house this voice said, '*I'm a-coming,*' and she went back in and this big, tall man followed her in the door. He had long hair, and long fingernails, and long teeth. So the old woman says, 'Why you got those long fingernails?' and he said, 'To dig graves with.' And she said, 'Why you got that long hair?' and he said, 'To lay graves with.' So then she said, 'Why you got those long teeth?'"

Henry's head leaned forward.

"To *EAT YOU UP!*"

Henry jumped, grinned. "Tell it again."

Henry stood on the stool at the woodstove. Uncle Jack handed him the salt shaker to sprinkle the two rabbits, each split down the middle, lying on a big piece of wax paper. In the big black frying pan, bacon grease was beginning to fizzle.

"Okay, I'm going to just drop them in there. Good. Now. We'll just wait till they're done, and then we can dress them up fancy. You can sit at the table now."

Uncle Jack cut open a lemon with the sharp kitchen knife.

When the rabbits were done on one side he turned them over with a fork, and then when they were done on that side he forked them to a plate and placed them in front of Henry at the table. "Now. We got all our stuff ready here. Get you a handful of them crushed pecans and sprinkle them on. Good. Now I'll pour this lemon juice in the frying pan, and let's let it heat for about a minute. Okay. Now. We stir it good. There you go. This is going to be good. Okay, I'm going to pour this over the rabbit, and we got a little scraped lemon peel I'm going to sprinkle on, then these real thin lemon slices. Now, don't that look good?

"Dorie. Dorie, come and get it. Come look what me and Henry cooked."

1939

―――

Three colored women dressed in white uniforms sat in the back of the trolley. Most of the other people were dressed up. Aunt Ruth, who was small, had let Caroline dress up in one of her dresses. Henry wore his coat and tie, and Aunt Dorie wore a Sunday dress. The trolley was so full that Henry sat in Dorie's lap.

"Is it like the museum in Raleigh?" Dorie asked Jack.

"Not exactly. You'll see."

"I'm just not sure about this." Somebody had loaned him a white jacket cut off at the waist. He was up to one of his schemes. The jacket and a little card he'd gotten from somewhere could get them all into the Electra — a special building that sometimes admitted only club members or high-priced ticket buyers. Jack was dressed as a cook, or waiter, a helper of some sort.

A low bridge crossed the channel, only wide enough for the trolley tracks, and Henry looked out at the water and boats. Tall masts with white sails and shiny wooden motorboats moved about. When the motorboats went fast, water slashed up from both sides in front.

"They might not ever open it up to cars," said Jack. "They're going to keep it special. And don't y'all be ashamed. We're as good as any of these people."

When they stepped down the trolley steps on Swan Island they were standing in a small station like the one they'd just left. The station was across the street from the house of the famous Papa John McNeill, the founder of McNeill, the town back across the channel. They could trolley around the island, but walking was cheaper.

They'd driven down in the truck that day, about an hour's drive, from Simmons to McNeill, then over on the trolley to Swan Island to see a building that would be all lit up with electricity, and to hear a big band that would play inside. It was a famous place, Uncle Jack said. Henry thought he'd be able to see water surrounding the island, but standing in the trolley station he couldn't see water anywhere. Jack asked a man in a uniform for directions. The man told them about five blocks and pointed. As they walked, Henry looked on the ground for wooden play blocks. After a while, he stared at the biggest building besides a city building he'd ever seen. It was three levels high, each of the top two levels a little less wide than the one below it, and on the very top was a tower with windows. He could hear music coming from inside. Uncle Jack led them up a wide set of stairs to a porch that went all the way around the building. A short line of people waited at a door. A bald-headed man sat behind a table. He waved at Jack.

"You-all wait right here for a minute," said Uncle Jack. He stood in line and handed the man a card when his time came. Then he motioned for them to come with him.

Inside was a large, open space with a shiny floor. At one end sat a raised stage with a giant clamshell behind it.

Four men on the stage played piano, guitar, bass fiddle, and trumpet. Caroline grabbed Henry's hand. Polished, dark wood columns stood around the large, open dance area. Red, white, and blue streamers hung from the ceiling. Electric lights brightened everything, and the late daylight shone through high windows in the west wall. As Henry looked up, he turned in a half circle.

Women and men stood talking. Some of the women had little clips holding back their shiny hair. The men wore coats and ties. No woman had a scarf on her head, and no man had on just a T-shirt. Some, holding small, thick glasses in their hands, occasionally glanced at Henry and Caroline.

Jack led them onto the porch. And there, just beyond a field of white sand, lay the ocean. Henry thought about Jesus walking on the sea, calming the waters during that terrible storm.

"Look," said Dorie. "Look at that screen. That's for a movie, ain't it?"

A big movie screen stood in the shallow surf. Men in

white coats were placing beach chairs on the beach between the Electra and the screen.

"Sure is," said Jack. "You-all go get some food. I need to do something over yonder." Inside, Henry, Caroline, and Aunt Dorie filled their plates with small red potatoes, string beans, fish that wasn't fried, small pieces of all-mixed-together lettuce and tomato and cucumber, and big rolls. They sat on the steps and ate together. Uncle Jack was setting up chairs. He turned and waved to them.

Henry watched and listened to the dressed-up people talk and laugh. He didn't see many other children except for three colored boys and a colored girl with their mama, who was dressed in white. He stepped back inside the door and watched as twenty or thirty men dressed in black suits prepared to make music. They moved with purpose and ease — like they might be from New York.

Then the music commenced: a fast song, a brass sound that filled every space in the room, drums in his chest. People took to the dance floor. Henry stood still. Caroline, Jack, and Dorie came in and stopped beside him. Caroline leaned against him.

When a slow, quieter song started, Jack took Dorie's hand and said, "Come on, honey. Let's give it a try."

"Jack, you know I can't dance."

"You know good and well there ain't nobody from the church all the way down here."

"I can't do it, Jack. I'm not supposed to."

"Well, you're going to watch the movie, ain't you?"

"Nobody's said anything about movies."

"Yet. They'll get to it."

As night came on, people wandered out to find seats on the beach and others gathered on the sand off to the side of the beach chairs. Henry, Caroline, Jack, and Dorie walked down the steps.

Jack said, "Let's leave our shoes under the steps."

"I'm wearing hose," said Dorie.

"So? Let's take off our shoes and socks, boys and girls."

Henry sat on the bottom step and pulled off his shoes and socks. He watched Aunt Dorie. She had turned her back and was taking off her stockings. He stuffed the socks into the shoes and felt the sand beneath his feet, cool.

Evening had calmed the ocean. They found a place near the beach chairs and sat on the sand without a blanket or quilt like some others had, and suddenly a bright light was thrown upon the movie screen and Henry followed the light back to its source — a machine he'd seen on a platform. A man stood behind the machine. The images on the screen were of men running across a field in a war and then of a big city. The main film then began, a story about a man in a fancy suit and a woman who almost had a halo. She had shiny earbobs and was either smiling or sad.

As they watched the movie, a gigantic, full, dull orange moon crept up out of the ocean as if to command armies, and people pointed at it, and Henry felt like it was so close that he could walk to the edge of the water and hold out his hands, palms up, and feel heat from the deep orange glow, then ride out in a rowboat along the path of reflections on the water, hold up an oar, and touch it, feel the oar against the crust.

The woman and the man were dancing up on the screen, and Jack said to him and Caroline, "Y'all sit right here," and he reached and pulled Dorie up by her hand. He led her over to a place on the beach that put the full moon right behind them, took her in his arms. They danced slow just like the people in the movie. They danced in front of the moon and then away and then back in front of it. Henry guessed that this might be the beginning of when Uncle Jack would not drink any more beers and Dorie would dance when Jack wanted to. He guessed that this was what his mama and daddy did before his daddy got hit by the timber.

"What are you thinking about?" asked Caroline.

"The moon."

"Me too. I was thinking about how it throws out beams of love that go into your heart."

"It's like it's alive and sad."

Caroline grabbed his arm, hard. "Look."

Aunt Dorie was motioning for them to come. She was standing with Uncle Jack and two men. The men pointed back toward the Electra, where two policemen talked to another man in a white coat. Uncle Jack jerked his arm from a policeman's hand. The policeman put his hand on the stick in his belt, and Uncle Jack kept talking.

Aunt Dorie walked toward him and Caroline now. She bent down and said, "We've got to go on out front and wait for Uncle Jack."

*   *   *

There was plenty of room on the trolley going back over to McNeill.

"Some people are going to look down on you no matter what," Uncle Jack said to Henry and Caroline. "But it takes a sorry son of a bitch to do it who's rich and in a club and got all he needs to get along and can run a big, fancy showplace like that and make more money than he can burn, and some of them don't even cut their own goddamn *grass!*"

"Jack, I don't think —"

"I'm going back over there," said Jack. The trolley was slowing to a stop. "And I guarantee you they'll know I was there. Here I bring my entire family, my niece and nephew and —"

"We got to get off, Jack."

"Chaps my ass. It just chaps my ass."

"Jack. They ought not to be hearing this."

"Oh yes they *had* ought to be hearing this."

Henry, Caroline, and Dorie were on the ground. Jack stepped down from the open door of the trolley, then sat down on the step. People stood behind him and then stepped around him. "That son of a bitch said white trash. I guess nobody ever called the Dampiers white trash," he said to Dorie.

"Jack, let's don't do this. Come on away from the trolley."

*   *   *

Henry and his cousin Carson, who'd come up from Florida on the train for a two-week visit, mashed the blackberries in water and painted streaks on their faces and circles on their stomachs and pulled loincloths tight up between their legs, fastened rope around their waists, and let the ends of the cloths fall. Then they ran for the woods down past Mrs. Albright's back porch. Henry had told Carson about the cats. Mrs. Albright was out beyond her backyard picking blackberries, and a few cats were along. She waved to the boys and they walked up to her.

"You're Henry's little cousin, ain't you?" Mrs. Albright said to Carson.

"Yes ma'am."

"Linda's boy?"

"Yes ma'am."

"Can you make the cats talk?" asked Henry.

"We might have to wait a minute or two," said Mrs. Albright. "That's Isaac, and that's John. The big John. Not John the Baptist. He's inside. Isaac, do you have something to say?"

"I thought you were *killing* Indians yesterday, boys," said Isaac.

Henry looked at Isaac. "We were, but today we're Navajo braves."

"Things switch around, I reckon, yes sir," said Isaac. "Do you boys know what the Germans are doing in Europe?"

"No," said Henry. He looked up at Mrs. Albright. "No sir."

"It's a shame," said Isaac.

"Well, well, well," said John. "Not everybody thinks so." John's ear twitched twice. He looked to the weeds at a butterfly and knelt, stalking.

Carson and Henry hid in ambush in the woods, then rode sidelong on pretend, gaudy-painted ponies, rising up at the last minute in terror-provoking splendor to shoot arrows — nails embedded in the ends of dried water reeds — into pine tree stumps, then whooped and hollered and charged into the bloody melee and scalped half-dead and stupefied soldiers with homemade tomahawks. Then rode off as reinforcements rode after them. They outran the reinforcements, hid, and slaughtered all of them too. And then scalped them.

The next afternoon Carson was Tom Mix and Henry was Johnny Mack Brown. They joined the U.S. Cavalry and sat in a tree and shot their air rifles and murdered over a hundred Indians, picking them off one by one, Indian braves who had foolishly camped in a narrow ravine.

Henry told Carson about the Electra, about all the lights, the big group of men who could every one play a musical instrument.

PART III

EXODUS

1950

In a wooded area just off a wagon path, Clearwater knelt on one knee, digging a hole with a broken jar. He'd just driven the Chrysler, while the boy, Henry, drove a stolen Oldsmobile a good distance ahead of him. They'd come from Cloverdale Springs Resort in Georgia to this spot near Treadlow, Georgia, clearly marked on a hand-drawn map. Henry was working out fine.

Henry felt good about his new job. It was easy, for one thing. Mr. Clearwater picked up the car from the criminal while Henry waited somewhere in the woods, or maybe behind a warehouse. Mr. Clearwater would drive up and get out of the stolen car, into his own car, and then Henry drove the stolen car, following a map to a place in the woods. They would bury stuff, switch license plates on the new car, transfer equipment, just like the regular thieves would have done. Mr. Clearwater knew a lot of hiding places and how to camouflage things. He'd been trained in the army and in the FBI and he kept records, maps, and all. And then they sold the car and Mr. Clearwater mailed the money to the FBI. Henry was paid in cash because they were undercover.

Henry was feeling kind of rich, and kind of comfortable, but still concerned about his Bible discoveries. And there was something not quite right about making money, a lot of money anyway, without working hard. It wasn't Christian somehow.

Mr. Clearwater finished digging the hole, then buried a billfold, papers, pencils, and two pairs of gloves from the glove compartment of the Oldsmobile.

The real robbers doing the actual stealing were sometimes in too big a hurry to do the little things that had to be done. Mr. Clearwater's job, and Henry's, Henry was learning, was to do exactly what criminals would do, else he and Clearwater might get caught, not by the law, but by somebody in the car-theft ring. The police would be no problem, of course, since Mr. Clearwater was in the FBI — they'd just let them go — but the criminals could get nasty.

Clearwater packed dirt with his hand, smoothed over the small mound with his fingertips, scattered leaves and pine straw over his work, stood and dusted the knees of his pants.

Henry leaned against the Olds, his hand on the fender,

waiting, sport coat sleeves too short, hair still standing up on top in back. "There's no tool like the fingers," he said.

"Yeah, that's right," said Clearwater.

Henry had had a chance to see some of the criminals down in Grover, Florida. They seemed like regular people. That showed how smart they were. One of the car painters had a gold tooth in front. Mr. Clearwater had said it was important for Henry not to talk to them.

Clearwater wiped each hand low on his pants in the rear, just above the cuff. "Go bring the Chrysler," he said. "Here's the keys." He tossed them.

Henry pulled the Chrysler up beside the Oldsmobile, turned off the ignition, got out. "I like them white-sidewall tires," he said. Mr. Clearwater was wiping his hands again.

Henry looked out across the field of broom straw that stood just beyond a few trees. The first stars of evening were beginning to show, and far across the field stood a long line of black pines. In the sky just above the pines lay a strip of yellow sky. It made him almost remember something he and Uncle Jack had done.

Clearwater opened the trunks of both cars so they could transfer the boy's belongings and some of his. He retrieved eight license plates from eight states; two crowbars; a fifth and half-fifth of Henry McKenna in a paper sack; a portable Royal typewriter in its case; a zip-up canvas bag containing two wigs, a hunting jacket, binoculars, two .38 pistols, a pearl-handled .32, masking tape, rope, three sticks of dynamite, blankets, and rubber dishwashing gloves.

He got out a clean white shirt and put it on, looked over at the place he'd buried the billfold and glove compartment contents. It looked good. He made an out-of-the-way incision in the Oldsmobile trunk lining and pushed the license plates through, then motioned for Henry, now standing there waiting like he ought to, to put his things in the trunk. Henry stepped over and placed his suitcase, valise, and a new cardboard box of Bibles in next to the spare tire.

Clearwater noticed a speck on his glasses. As he wiped it off, he saw that it was a dark red. If you found the sweet spot above and behind the ear there wasn't much trouble if you could swing hard with both hands — real quick. Knocked them out cold. But if you missed it and had to hit him again . . . not good. They'd be ducking and moving all around, and you sometimes couldn't be accurate, might get a little spatter. He didn't like to use the crowbar that way. He could kill somebody. Misuse of tools. That's what his pistols were for. He'd killed with pistol, rifle, bayonet, and piano wire in France six years before and had experienced the luck of having bullets hit all around him but never touch him, and he'd experienced the weakness in his knees and the tingle in his chin just as he witnessed life leave somebody. You had to do your job. It was a job. And *this* was a job, just at a different place and time, all in the same world, a world that was no more than a place for things to happen. If your job brought wealth, then good.

"Okay, I'll follow you this time," said Clearwater. "I'll drive the Chrysler. And remember, if we get split up, pull over and let *me* find *you*."

They drove along in the night on a two-lane blacktop for about an hour, meeting few cars. Henry thought about home. It wouldn't be too long before he could save up enough money to buy a car. He might could buy Caroline one too, or Aunt Dorie. Or maybe one for both of them. He might get a chance after six months or so to join the FBI as a regular G-man. Mr. Clearwater hadn't mentioned it, but for sure that's what would come next. He'd have to tell Carson. Maybe he could even arrange for Carson to come to work for the FBI too.

They stopped at a service station and filled up with gas. Clearwater took the lead for the final short stretch. As he drove, he pulled a letter from his pocket, turned on the inside light, and read directions. He looked at the map and then up to the road. In a few minutes he turned onto a gravel road and then into the driveway of a house with a large, two-story garage out back. People there would have information on any new options he might have. He went in, then came back out and explained to Henry that the Oldsmobile would be painted within twelve hours and they'd be on their way. They would spend the night in a room attached to the garage.

Henry sat in the chair beside his bed. "How did you find out about this place?" he asked.

"It's all arranged beforehand." Clearwater took off his shirt, folded it and placed it in his suitcase, turned back the covers on his bed. "They are very well organized, and it's all made up of several branches."

"Will they know you're the one that turned them in? That you're the spy?"

Clearwater brought his finger to his mouth, shook his head.

Henry nodded. "I need to know where I can have some Bibles mailed to. I need to order some. Is there a place we'll be staying for a while?"

"We'll be back and forth through Atlanta right much. That's where we'll be heading tomorrow." Clearwater was in bed on his back. He turned onto his side. "I want to go to sleep."

"Did you know there were two different stories about the beginning of the world in Genesis?"

"No."

"I don't see how they can both be wrote by the same God."

Clearwater turned onto his back, came up onto his elbows, pulled back the covers, and swung his feet to the floor. "I guess I'll have me a little drink. You want one?"

"I don't see why not."

Clearwater produced the bottle. "See if there ain't some glasses in that cabinet."

Henry found two glasses, the bright-colored aluminum kind with the turned-out lip. He had to tell somebody about all this Genesis stuff, and having a little drink would be a way to get Mr. Clearwater talking.

"Get you some water if you want to mix it," said Clearwater as he poured the drinks.

"Uncle Jack always drunk it outen the bottle."

Mr. Clearwater handed him a glass.

Henry smelled the whiskey, sloshed it around in his glass, took a sip. It almost burned. "What kind of church were you raised in?" he asked.

"It was called something, but I don't remember. I was pretty little."

Henry started taking off his pants.

"Won't that belt end fit through a loop?" asked Clearwater.

"Oh, yeah. I guess so."

"Could you see if it will."

Henry fastened back his pants, checked the belt. "It does."

"Good. One more thing. You think you could get a hat or some hair oil to keep your hair down in back like I asked you?"

"My daddy's hair was like this is what my Aunt Dorie always told me," said Henry as he touched his hair. "I just like to use water on my hair."

"Yeah, I know. Now I need to go to sleep."

The next morning as they stood inside the paint shop near an adding machine on a low table, Henry saw Clearwater pick up a nickel and a dime from the floor and pocket them. He wondered how he might bring up his concerns about the Bible again. Then while taking a leak in the bathroom, he noticed a penny *in the urinal.* As he came out, Clearwater went in. When Clearwater came out, Henry returned — just to see. The penny was gone. Did he put chewing gum on the end of a pencil and then drop the penny in the sink and wash it?

Outside, they looked at the fresh green paint on the Oldsmobile.

"Looks pretty good, don't it?" said Clearwater.

"Sure does. It looks like it's been painted for a while or something."

"That's right. They age it with damp cloths and this fine sand that comes from somewhere in Arizona."

On the road, Henry fit his fingers into the scallops of the Oldsmobile steering wheel. He followed the Chrysler. They stopped at a used-car dealer's lot in downtown Thomasville, Georgia, far south of Atlanta. And when he came out Clearwater gave Henry his two tens and a five-dollar bill.

That afternoon as they rode together, Clearwater told Henry to stop just beyond, but out of sight of, the Night's Rest Motel in Jeffries, Georgia, about five miles southwest of Atlanta. Henry would walk in and Clearwater would drive in, as usual. But before Henry got out of the car, Clearwater told him they'd take a two-day rest, and that he'd be driving into Atlanta to observe some criminal activity.

"Can I come?" asked Henry.

"I need to do it myself."

*   *   *

Henry sat on the bed in his room. It felt hard and the springs creaked. Tomorrow he'd go out for a serious day of Bible selling. He might iron one of his suits. The woman at the desk probably had an iron. A floor lamp stood in the corner, and a lightbulb on a cord hung from the middle of the room. Maybe he would go take a shower. One had been advertised on a sign in the office. He took off his suit and hung it and his sport coat on hangers in the wardrobe.

He walked to his window and looked down the road. A roadside fruit stand. He washed his face and hands, decided to postpone the shower, dressed in his underwear and second suit, picked up his valise, and walked out to the road. The air was hot and humid, and the sun was behind a heavy cloud in the west. The fruit stand was maybe fifty yards down the road, under a couple of funeral home tents, it looked like, white plywood bins all around. The paint was thin enough to see through to the plywood, even from far away. A big hand-painted sign, black paint on the white paint, said SQUASH, FRUIT, TURNIPS, CANNED GOODS, JELLY AND ECT. Somebody sat in there behind a table, beside a hanging scale. He would sell a Bible or two. They'd have cash on hand.

When he got up close he saw it was a girl, a kind of big-boned, blond, curly-headed girl with a dress so thin it seemed to show her skin beneath. The curls dropped around her face. As he stepped under the tent, thunder sounded far off. A chilled breeze came up.

The girl nodded and smiled, said hello, threw up her hand. He glanced over the baskets of squash, apples, tomatoes, shelves of canned string beans, cranberries, beets, tomatoes, jelly. She was kind of pretty. He *liked* a nose with a hump in it, and her lips were big, kind of like a colored girl's lips. He'd never told anybody that he liked the way a lot of colored girls looked. He glanced up and down the road and down the wagon path that led away behind the stand, probably to a house or farm where maybe she lived.

She was reading a big book. He couldn't see the title. He picked up a peach, pressed it with his thumb, picked up another two.

"Where'd you get peaches and apples and tomatoes this time of year?"

"Oh, we got a hothouse for the tomatoes, and a truck stops by with some fruit and other stuff."

He stepped up to the table. A closed cigar box sat beside four books and a stack of paper sacks. "I reckon I want a few peaches," he said.

She looked up and smiled, picked up a bag, held it open for him. "They're mighty good," she said. "I just ate one myself."

"Do you wash off the fuzz?" he asked.

"I *wipe* it off while I run water on it. That's a odd question."

"I didn't see no water around was why I thought about it."

"There's some in that bucket over there."

Henry looked. He'd forgotten he was selling Bibles. "My aunt always made me wash off the fuzz, and then once I got more or less growed up I started eating them with the fuzz on. It was supposed to make you itch, but it never itched me that I know of."

She placed the bag in the hanging scale tray.

"That looks like about eight cents," she said. "I'll take a nickel, though. I'm Marleen Green, and I'm pleased to meet you." She put out her hand.

She was kind of pert and *forward,* by golly, and he saw the *it* — not there in every girl's face, something to do with the way she looked at him, and then too it had something to do with the little dimple in her cheek, and the dip under her nose that seemed to pull her upper lip up just a tiny bit in a way that made a slight urge drop from his head into his chest, arms, on down. He reached a hand across the table. "Pleased to meet you. I'm Henry Dampier."

She squeezed his hand nicely.

"Do you mind if I sit down?" he said. He couldn't have cared less about selling a Bible.

"Nothing would make me happier. I'm not doing much business."

He thought: And the evening and the morning were the first day. "My aunt and uncle had a garden every year. My aunt still does, and my sister's helping her out."

"What kind of work are you in? Architecture?"

"Architecture?"

"I like to say odd things. I asked a woman in here yesterday if she was going to the memorial service and she looked at me funny. 'Aluminum' is a funny word too. If I ever bought a parrot I'd teach him to say 'aluminum' when somebody sneezed. Anyway, you look real smart, and I just read a book about architecture, about this man named Frank Lloyd Wright and all the ideas he had. He tried to fit any house he built to the habits of who it was for, and then a crazy man burned down his house, Wright's house, and killed his wife with an ax. Idn't that just awful? What kind of work *do* you do?"

"I'm a Bible salesman. It's kind of a second job. I work for the government too. Killed his wife with an *ax?* Where'd you read that?"

"A book from the library. They have a bookmobile that comes through here every two weeks. The man with the ax was their cook."

"Gosh."

"I guess he got inhabited. I hope you're not a census taker. My cousin shot a census taker and had to go to prison. That's not your government job, is it?"

"Oh no, I'm not one of those. It's something I'm not supposed to talk about."

"You can trust me, but I won't ask you any questions. Do you know what *e-t-c* stands for?"

"Et cetera. And so forth."

"A lot of people don't know that. My brother couldn't even spell it, and he put that 'and' in front of it. I'm going to paint over it. He didn't go past sixth grade. My mama didn't go past sixth grade either, but she can spell better than I can. How long have you been a Bible salesman?"

"Not too long. I started in the spring. And the government stuff I just started a few weeks ago." Henry had never met a girl so full of words and talk and interesting all at the same time. He bet he could talk to her about Genesis. "Do you go to church?" He took a bite out of a peach.

"Not anymore. A lady came to my house and took me to Trinity Baptist, up the road there, three or four times when I was twelve, and then they brought us some canned food right before Christmas and it made my daddy so mad he wouldn't let me go back." She raised her eyebrows and smiled. "I don't know if he'd let me buy a Bible or not."

He shook his head. "I'm not here to sell you a Bible, necessarily. In fact, I didn't mean to get into all that. My main thing these days is my heart condition." Where had *that* come from? The Bible salesman with yellow socks — up at Calhoun Crossing, in the mountains — kept talking about his heart condition. He'd had a Bible with a cutout place for a whiskey flask, and he had all these stories. "I don't mean to get into all that, either. I'll tell you one thing, them peaches are mighty good."

"They *are* good peaches. What kind of heart condition?"

"They don't know. Can't figure it out. Sometimes I get real weak and have to sit down for a spell, or lay down. I have to lay down right much." Why was he lying?

"I'm sorry to hear that."

"Yeah, the doctor — actually there were three doctors, up in Durham, North Carolina, at Duke Hospital — and they told me I might not live as long as most people, but I don't aim to let that slow me down none." He needed to stop.

"Do you have any hobbies?" she asked.

"Hobbies?"

"Yeah, you know, hobbies."

"I, ah, collect exotic cards."

"What kind?"

"Pictures. Kind of like postcards." This is it, thought Henry. She's the one. She seems like she's in love with me. This is where I need to just go ahead and go ahead. "I got these cards in my room up at the motel, right up there." He pointed to the motel. Jump in, jump in. Abraham did. "If you want to come up and see them, I'm going to be around for another day or so."

"I'd better not. My daddy got in a fight with Mr. Sawyer, the man that runs the place up there. But I've got a book from England that you can open up and castles will pop up. I could bring it here to the stand tomorrow, if you want to come see it. We live down that wagon path back there. And I got some poems too. That's my hobby, writing poetry. I'll be here at three-thirty."

"I'll be selling Bibles, probably, but I'll make time."

They sat and talked and laughed — she laughed a lot. He told her about the cat and snake burial. She told stories about her little brother. He had painted some baby kittens with house paint, and poured molasses in her daddy's shoes, and tried to hitchhike to Atlanta.

A car stopped and two women bought jelly, canned beets, and tomatoes.

As Marleen talked and laughed and then looked Henry right in the eye, he realized he'd be twenty years old when he got his first sex relation. That seemed about right, given all he'd been learning from the Bible. He could . . . it was just all over him, in his throat and heart and hands.

Then he told her about his Uncle Jack, about him leaving Aunt Dorie and how sad he was, how sad she'd been. About Aunt Dorie later marrying his Uncle Samuel, the good part of that being his cousin Carson coming to live with him.

The next afternoon, Clearwater was gone, researching, and Marleen and Henry sat in the fruit stand and looked at the pop-up book resting in her lap.

"They just pop right up, don't they?" said Henry.

"They sure do."

Henry could feel her thigh warm against his as just the slightest wisp of wet air, dewlike, was blown in from the slow rain. "Are you sure you can't come up and see my cards tonight?" he asked her.

"I don't think so. I don't like Mr. Sawyer. But if you come down that wagon path right after dark, I'll meet you, because I can say I'm going up to my sister's to spend the night. It looks like it's going to clear up."

To spend the night. To spend the night. To spend the night. The heavens had opened, the floodgates were asunder. He would "go in unto" her. Within hours. "That's good. That's good. I'll meet you. We'll do something." His breathing had picked up.

"Don't go past the little bridge over the creek," she said.

"Right after dark."

"Right after dark."

He started singing "Yankee Doodle" on the walk back to his room, where he was supposed to meet Clearwater before dinner, and there Clearwater was, waiting in a lawn chair. He stood. "Pack up," he said. "We got to move."

"Now?"

Clearwater nodded toward a new car near Henry's room, a black Packard. "We got to get that car on out of here."

"But I've got an appointment, kind of."

"We got to move it. Now."

"Can I —"

"Let's go. I'll follow you in the Chrysler."

"I was thinking —"

"We're going to a paint shop in South Carolina. The maps are in there. Look them over and let's get going."

"Could I just stop by that fruit stand down —"

"*Fruit stand?* Have you lost your damn mind?"

Henry quickly packed his suitcase and loaded it and his valise into the backseat of the stolen car. What would she think? Maybe she had a telephone. He'd call information. A Mr. Green. What road, what route?

The map led Henry to a paint shop in Caleb, South Carolina, about two hours northeast of Jeffries. As long as he called her before dark everything would be okay. They left the new car, and Clearwater dropped Henry off a hundred yards or so from the Spangler Motel. The sun was setting.

At the front desk he asked the lady if he could call information on her phone. And if he got a number could he call it and pay her for the charges. She said fine. He called information. No Greens were listed in Jeffries. He asked the operator if she could give him the address of the Night's Rest Motel in Jeffries. She said she wasn't supposed to give out addresses but she could if it was some kind of emergency. He said it was an emergency. The address was Route 6. He'd write her a postcard.

Clearwater was waiting outside at a picnic table when Henry started for his room. The place they'd meet for breakfast, he said, was across the road — Rita's Café. "What took you so long?" asked Clearwater.

"I needed to make a call."

"That fruit stand?"

Henry looked at him.

"You found you a woman down there, didn't you?"

"I think I did."

"Did you get you some snatch?"

"Not yet."

In his room at a small desk with a lamp, sitting in his underwear, an oscillating fan on the dresser turning its face one way and then the other, Henry penciled a message on a piece of notebook paper, erased, penciled, erased, and then wrote in ink on one of several postcards he'd bought on the way out of Cloverdale Springs.

Dear Marleen, Hello from the archetect (sp?). Ha Ha. I am very sorry that I didn't make it back to see you tonight. I got called away on business. It was serious business or I wouldn't have left out like I did. I can explain it to you when I come back to see you which is something I'm planning to do as soon as I can get a way to do it. I really want to come back. In the meantime you can write to me in care of general delivery in Atlanta. I was really looking forward to seeing you tonight. I am really sorry. More soon.

Sincerely Yours,

Henry Dampier

The next morning at breakfast, Henry wanted to talk about her — but the words wouldn't come. He wasn't proud of his intentions, somehow. He didn't know how to explain what was going on. There was this big mix of falling in love and his first "go in unto." All at the same time. Marleen, Marleen. Marleen Green.

After Clearwater sold the freshly painted car, they headed south toward Florida in the Chrysler, Henry driving.

Clearwater sat in the passenger seat, studying maps. He always fiddled with maps. Maps of mountains, rivers, showing little circles for heights and depths. He reached around an open map, changed the radio station a few times, landed in the middle of a song. "Do you know who that is singing?" he asked.

"Nope."

"Roy Acuff. I used to know him in Knoxville. We messed around some together, played music. He ran for governor a few years ago."

"What did you play?"

"Instrument?"

"Yessir."

"Guitar."

"You still play?"

"I quit."

"Why?"

"I just did. It wadn't very profitable."

"Where's Knoxville?"

"Knoxville, Tennessee. You don't know Knoxville is in Tennessee?"

"I didn't take any geography for some reason," said Henry. He was eating a banana. He thought about Marleen. She would know. "I know all about Hank Williams, though."

Clearwater had trouble with the way Henry peeled only an inch or so of the banana, then nibbled. And how could somebody with their head out their ass not know about Roy Acuff? "Why don't you just peel the whole thing and eat it?"

Henry rolled down the window and threw out his banana peel. "That's just the way I do it. I don't like to touch the thing itself."

They were driving by a wide, bare field that seemed snow-white under the full moon now high in the sky. Henry didn't see how he could talk about Marleen. He was going to be a perfect assistant to Mr. Clearwater, quiet and obedient, and then he'd sure enough have a big job. He could probably go back to Washington, DC, for meetings and stuff. He'd only been the one time — with the safety patrol in the eighth grade.

They stopped for a blinking red light, just south of New Bilbow, Georgia. The radio news said the Night Shooter had just shot another motorist between the eyes up somewhere in North Carolina. They still hadn't caught him.

"Turn in there and let's get a bite to eat," said Clearwater.

Henry turned into the parking lot of the Piggy Pot Diner.

"You want a nip of whiskey?" asked Clearwater.

"Sure."

Inside, they waited at their table for food. Clearwater said, "I met that guy, the Night Shooter, right before he escaped."

"What's his real name?"

"Skipper Thurston was all I ever heard."

"How'd you know him?"

"I met him in the county jail in Thomasville, Georgia. When I had to put some people in jail down there." Clearwater visualized the glasses, the face, the teeth, his look when you were talking to him, a look that said he was somewhere else, not there. "He was a trusty back then. I talked to him for a little bit." Clearwater remembered how the Night Shooter didn't want you to see how his hand shook when he held something.

"What was he like?"

"Not what you'd think. He was kind of nervous. He had real fine teeth. He reminded me of my mama in a funny way. Kind of sensitive or something. Short fuse."

"My granddaddy had false teeth," said Henry. "Me and my sister spent the night over there one time, and I got his false teeth out of a glass of water and put them in my mouth over top of mine. They fit right over my teeth, and everybody laughed except Pa D. That was his nickname. At first he didn't even recognize them. Aunt Dorie did, though. And Aunt Dorie was always telling me to take care of widows and orphans because it was in the Bible. Kind of like your mama, I guess. She'd send me to take blankets down to this widow woman that lived down below us. She had a retarded son and about a hundred cats. That could talk."

"The son?"

"The cats. The widow was Mrs. Albright, and she'd throw her voice to the cats. Especially around kids, but she'd do it by herself too, sitting out on her porch."

The waitress, wearing a white apron and a white paper hat, walked up with a plate in each hand, looking at one, then the other. "Who had the pork chops?"

"I did," said Henry.

When she walked away, Henry said the blessing. "Dear God, for these and all thy blessings we are grateful. Amen."

Clearwater looked at him while he prayed. He'd keep him for a while. "There's this cabin camp we can stop at for a few days. Up in Brownlee, on the Okaloga River. You'll get to meet Blinky. He's an old buddy. He spent some time with me and Roy Acuff. We had some good times. Then he got recruited by the FBI too, and he pretends he's running this company up in McNeill."

"And we'll have a few days off?"
"That's right."
Marleen, Marleen. Marleen Green.
"Did Blinky play an instrument?" asked Henry.
"Naw. He was a promoter. You'll see when you meet him."

The next morning, as they passed through Stint, Georgia, Henry mailed two postcards:

Dear Aunt Dorie, This postcard picture is where I just stayed. I'm having some real adventures. I've got a new job except I'm still selling Bibles too. I can tell you about it when I see you. I'm working with a real nice man. I have been staying true to God, spreading his holy word, and have been praying faithfully. Tell Caroline I'll write her a letter next time. Out of room.

Truly yours,
Henry

Dear Carson, How are you. I am doing fine. I'm in on a deal. I can't tell you anything about it though. Let's just say it has something to do with the government and is pretty interesting, and I'm working with this man who is really smart. I don't know when I'll get home. We might do some work up at McNeill and

Swan Island, though. I'll let you know when. Out of room to write.

Your cuz,

Henry

At the Okaloga River Cabin Camp, Henry sat on a rock wall along the outside of a bend that brought water straight toward him and then took it away. The river was swollen from rains and brought debris from upriver. He was thinking about two things: Marleen and the Bible. He'd been reading a Bible lately that was different from the Bible he'd been reading growing up. And the one he was now reading was the real one. He'd only dip-read the first one. That dip-reading had something to do with the big problem he had now, he was thinking. The big bright cloud that was his belief, delivered by the Bible and Sunday school and Antioch Baptist Church and Preacher Gibson and Aunt Dorie, seemed smaller and less white than it once was.

That night, sitting on his screened-in porch with a lamp cord through his window, he read into the New Testament, looking for stories about wine and sin. He read verses about sin in the books of Acts and Timothy, and figured out that the wine Jesus was drinking was not grape juice or they would have called it that. Grape juice wouldn't have been making people drunk. People had called Jesus a drunk. Where was that? Matthew 11:19. Why was that in the Bible? Jesus was drinking wine for sure. He made it hisself. No reason to think it was grape juice, unfermented, like Preacher

Gibson said. It was okay for him to have a drink with Mr. Clearwater. All those people getting drunk in the Old Testament. There had been so many of them. Were Henry's thoughts about women and girls and all that, were they sin? Just his thoughts about it? Well, Jesus said it was, it looked like, so he'd gotten to looking for stuff that Jesus said, and he came up in Matthew 19:12 on that about somebody being born a eunuch. That had to be a fairy because a eunuch was a castrated man. Why had Jesus told all about a fairy and *not* had a problem with it?

Then he read in Timothy 2:14 that Adam wasn't responsible for sin, but he remembered differently. So he went searching. First Timothy 2:14 said, "And Adam was not deceived, but the woman being deceived was in the transgression."

He turned straight back to Genesis and found that God blamed both of them and the snake too, which was supposed to be the devil in disguise, but what the actual snake had to do with it wasn't clear, *but he got punished,* and that couldn't make sense, any sense at all, because animals didn't reason things through like people. The snake hadn't had a chance, hadn't had a *choice,* and then it said that Adam would return to dust. Why wouldn't he go to heaven or hell? That's where everybody went, wasn't it? Nobody just returned to dust, did they? Was there not a heaven when Adam was alive? Wait, in Genesis 1:1 God created heaven and earth; so there *was* a heaven when he told Adam he was going back to dust, but God hadn't created hell. Did he create hell? It didn't *say* so. Did he just think about it down the line? That didn't sound like somebody "all-knowing." And there was the "and I will dwell in the house of the Lord for ever" in the Old Testament — that was heaven, wasn't it? Another problem was that you couldn't dwell in the house of the Lord like David said he would without accepting Jesus, but Jesus hadn't been born yet. How was that supposed to work out? Why hadn't any of this been handled in church, where it ought to have been handled? Was it a secret? Did Caroline know? Did Carson know? "The Lord is my shepherd, I shall not want. He maketh me to lie down in green pastures . . ." Now *this* seemed almost like it was about a different kind of God. The Lord. The Lord seemed kind of like a *mama* might be.

He couldn't now — in a prayer — get beyond the words "Dear God." He thought to pray to Jesus instead of God. "Dear Jesus, please guide and direct me. Please answer my prayer. Please give me some kind of understanding about what's wrote down in the Bible."

He thought about Marleen. Marleen, Marleen. Marleen Green. He thought about walking over to Mr. Clearwater's door, knocking, and when he came to the door, saying, "Ma'am, I've got something real pretty in a little box here I'd like to show you if you wouldn't mind me coming in just a minute," and maybe Clearwater would laugh. And then Henry could ask him if he could borrow his car. Naw. It wouldn't work. He'd better not. Clearwater probably wouldn't even laugh. He looked like Clark Gable with big ears, but he acted kind of like . . . President Truman. Not very juicy at all.

*   *   *

Blinky Smathers was five feet tall — five feet even. He usually wore a little flat British hat with a top that flopped forward onto the short bill. His big red face was square, his eyebrows came together in the middle, and his eyes bulged out. He didn't talk — rather, he barked, hoarsely. As if he were six feet tall, he strode toward Clearwater, grabbed his hand, reached up, slapped him on the shoulder, and growled, "It's good to see you, Bucky. On the muddy Okaloga. I got a hour or two." Another man, wearing sunglasses, sat in the open driver's door of Blinky's Cadillac, picking at a wildflower, letting the pieces drop one by one.

"Is he going to stay in the car?" asked Clearwater.

"He's not the talky type."

In a few minutes, Blinky and Clearwater faced each other, sitting in rocking chairs on the small porch of Clearwater's cabin.

"Do you want me to send you somebody to help you out?" asked Blinky. "Or do you want to keep the boy for these next two?"

"He's okay. So far."

"You know I'd like to do it myself, but I just can't afford to get mixed up in it no more."

"I know," said Clearwater.

"Too much to look after. Way too busy."

"Yeah, I know, and it's getting bigger all the time, ain't it?"

"Oh yeah. I want you up at the top with me, Bucky, right

there beside me — just like in that first jeep." Blinky held up the freshly lit tip of his cigar and looked at it. "You remember that — you riding my back so we wouldn't have but one set of footprints?"

"Of course I remember it."

"God, what fun. If they paid any attention to them footprints in that mud, they said, 'Whoa. That was one heavy son of a bitch.' Huh?"

"Yeah."

"Now. Okay — this new stuff, two safes, I'm keeping off the sheets. I can do that every once in a while. Just you and me and Teddy Lamont know about it. You remember Teddy. He's the mole on this first gig, close to Panakala, Florida, at a plantation. I've drawn up a rough plan. You can smooth it out. A Sunday morning gig. Teddy will have some women in on it Saturday night for the hired hands around there. He's assured me the coast'll be clear. We'll have to take the whole safe — with a forklift and dump truck — or at least you'll have the forklift if you need it. The safe's full of secret compartments. We're lucky to have that truck and forklift, Bucky. They've come in handy. The mark, a Greenlove out of New York, you may have heard of him, will never report it missing. He can't afford to. We know that. I'll take a train down here to see the family. You'll deliver the safe to me — right here at the cabin camp — and I'll drive it back in the truck, get it open at the plant. You can follow me up there if you want to. But you know you can trust me. We'll do a sixty-forty split. You decide what you want to pay the boy."

"Sixty-forty which way?"

Blinky laughed. "Aw, Bucky. You're still funny. Still funny. Now, the second gig is just as big, I think, but different. A doctor. We don't need the safe. Just what's in it. You can decide how to get him to open it. Straight job. The G-boys are about to start an investigation. Down in Drain. But the doc don't know they're after him. You know Drain?"

"Oh yeah."

"The truck and forklift is already scheduled for you to pick up in McNeill." Blinky handed Clearwater a folder. "It's all in there. Get up there early and spend a little time on Swan Island. Nice beaches."

"What's the doctor's name — in Drain?" asked Clearwater.

"Criddenton. Loaded. Absolutely. He's got guys coming in from all over for face operations, bullet removal, on and on. Does abortions."

Henry, walking from a shower in the bathhouse, saw the Cadillac and knew it must be Blinky's. Somebody was in the driver's seat and somebody on Clearwater's porch. If there was some way he could get a ride with these guys up to Jeffries, maybe . . . No, he'd better not ask about that. He needed to act right since Blinky was higher up than Clearwater. The guy in the driver's seat didn't seem like the FBI. He seemed like a truck driver with a suit and tie. He wouldn't even look up.

On the porch, Blinky grabbed Henry's hand, reached up, slapped him on the shoulder. "So this is the young man I've heard so much about," he growled. "We're proud of all you're doing for us. Cigar?" His lower eyelids were red, like a hound dog's.

"Thank you," said Henry. "My uncle used to smoke Rum Crooks."

"Good cigar," said Blinky. "Cheap, but good." He glanced at Clearwater, slapped Henry on the shoulder again. "Right?"

It wasn't a question — it was a command of some sort. FBI? Blinky wasn't what he'd pictured.

Henry took the cigar handed him, and then the box of kitchen matches Blinky offered from his pants pocket. "Thank you," he said.

"I like a big match," said Blinky. "Anybody ever show you how to light a match in a thirty-knot wind?"

"Nosir."

"Well, before I leave out of here, I'll teach you. Or if I forget, you get Bucky there to show you. Mr. Clearwater. You can still do it, can't you, Bucky?"

"Sure can."

Bucky? thought Henry. Bucky? Well, of course. They're undercover agents.

"We had a sergeant," said Blinky. "Sergeant Dunlevel, that taught us, huh, Bucky?"

"Right."

"Dunlevel would as soon hit you upside the head as look at you. Pull up that chair," he said to Henry. "We've got a couple of unusual jobs coming up. Mr. Hoover is very interested. We're basically dismantling the criminal element of the East Coast of the United States — from the inside. There'll be some reward in it for you down the line — in more ways than one. And I understand you're a Christian?"

"Yes sir."

"What denomination?"

"Baptist."

"Baptist. Ah, Baptist. Sweet word. Baptist. You ever heard of 'Between the Sheets'?"

"No sir."

"Add 'Between the Sheets' to the name of a hymn. 'I Surrender All . . . Between the Sheets.'"

Henry caught on, laughed. "'Love Lifted Me Between the Sheets.'"

"That's it," barked Blinky. "There's some good ones." He looked at Clearwater, who was smiling with half his mouth. "*You* go to church, don't you, Bucky?"

"Not much," said Clearwater.

"I was raised upstream," said Blinky to Henry, pointing his cigar. "Come down here from North Carolina once in a while to visit the family. Mr. Hoover appreciates the work you're doing for us, son. This is going to be big when it breaks. But listen." He took a puff, blew a smoke ring that rolled up toward the ceiling. He looked at Henry kind of hard. "Don't tell nobody what you're doing. Nobody. That would be unwise." He looked out at the Cadillac like he'd heard something. "I got to get on the road. You boys keep up the good work. It's an important mission." He stood, turned, looked at Henry. "This gig down in Florida — big fish, big fish. We've got to get the goods on this guy before we arrest him. We arrest him now, our whole operation falls through. We get his *goods,* he'll think one of his rivals done it and then . . . well, then we're sowing seeds of *discord.* Huh?" He raised his eyebrows, smiled. "'Holy, Holy, Holy Between the Sheets'? Huh?" He lifted his hand with the cigar, headed for his Cadillac and driver. "Stay out of trouble, boys."

That night Henry, in his cabin, dreamed about Uncle Jack again. He'd started dreaming about him soon after he left Aunt Dorie. At first he told Aunt Dorie about the dreams, but then after Aunt Linda died and Aunt Dorie married Uncle Samuel, he stopped telling her about them. In this dream, they were walking along a wagon path to check rabbit boxes. Uncle Jack was striding fast and Henry was skipping along, trying to keep up, and Uncle Jack suddenly stopped, turned, squatted, laughed, grabbed both sides of Henry's head and shook. Uncle Jack's teeth were all gold, and the shaking made Henry's neck tickle. Henry woke up laughing or dreaming he was laughing. He couldn't tell which.

The next morning, he felt full of energy. Uncle Jack never saw a sad day in his life. Henry thought again about asking Clearwater to let him borrow his car. It wasn't that far back to Jeffries. But he'd say no, and he'd realize something was up.

He dressed in his black suit, filled his valise with Bibles. He had picked up a box of free Bibles at the post office in

Atlanta, general delivery, sent from the New Visions Bible Society in Boston. He tried on his new fedora in front of the mirror in his room, placed it toward the back of his head and then more forward and at an angle.

He stopped by the camp office and left two letters to be mailed. The first was his form letter, with only the names, dates, and places changed.

Dear Mr. Humphries,

I take pen to paper hoping this epistle finds you in good times. I am a traveling preacher of the Gospel (Missionary Baptist) and I appreciate the work the Heritage Bible Society is doing for everybody by distributing the Word of God free of charge. What a valuable contribution to our sinful society! I am a young man, twenty years of age, just starting in on a circuit ministry that will take me to Missionary Baptist churches and also other churches and tent meetings and house meetings throughout North Carolina, South Carolina, and Georgia.

I am doing all I can to support widows and orphans as directed by the holy scripture and when I am in a better financial predicament I will be able to make contributions to your organization for sure.

If you can send a box or two of Bibles I am presently in Atlanta, Georgia, until sometime in July. Mail can be sent through General Delivery. I am very sure that I could give away 50 Bibles in a short while to very needy people who are hungry for God's word and do not have the money handy to afford a Bible.

May God Bless You,
Henry Dampier

Dear Caroline,

Everything is going as usual. I'm sorry I haven't wrote in so long. I sold seven Bibles yesterday and I am finding that a lot of housewives want a new Bible. We are headed back down through Atlanta, Georgia. Send me a letter when you all get the phone and a phone number so I can call. Mr. Clearwater the man I am traveling with has a pistol and we shot two squirrels yesterday and I fixed squirrel stew in this motel with little kitchens in the rooms. We had some chili peppers from a store in Marietta, Georgia. It was real good and Mr. Clearwater had not ever eaten any squirrel. I had lots of canned vegetables mixed in so it was not as good as it could be.

Next time I write I will write Aunt Ruth and Ma D. Tell them that. I hope we can come before too long to see you all. Write back when you can. This time send mail to Atlanta Ga. General Delivery.

I will let you know when we will be coming up to Swan Island. If there's any way you could plan a vacation in Swan Island and bring Carson that would be great. Glenn could come too. I hope you and him are still getting along dandy. I forgot to mention him last time I wrote. Please tell him hello. I might not get a chance to drive home because of my new work which is too complicated to write out (plus I am not supposed to tell). What this means is I might not get the time to come to Simmons this time but will be coming to Swan Island for sure.

Love & Kisses,
Henry

I'm not so concerned with what <u>you</u> know and say and how <u>you</u> behave, although that is very important. . . . I'm interested in how the <u>customer</u> behaves. Because her behavior will lead her to buy or it will lead her to refuse to buy. You're a leader, a guide, a mover, a maker, a teacher, a chief, a molder, a baker. And if you don't have a lot of confidence, you need to pretend you do.

At about noon Henry returned to a house just up the road from the cabin camp. He'd passed it up that morning because it looked like not only a good sell stop but a good dinnertime stop. It had hanging flowers on the porch and was a good bit back from the road. He fastened his top shirt button, tightened his tie, and pulled his coat sleeves down as far as he could, tipped his hat back a bit so he wouldn't look like a gangster. As he walked up the driveway, he noticed a black DeSoto, 1939, in the garage beside the house — facing outward. Looked a little dusty.

It was good to get under the porch roof, out of the heat.

He knocked, stepped back a few steps. A lady with a hair bun on top and crochet needles stuck through it answered the door. She was bent a little. As she pushed open the screen, Henry removed his hat and held it across his chest. He noticed that she had a little mole on her chin that looked like the tip end of a fishing worm. She had a twinkle in her eye and held a white table napkin in her hand. He felt confident about an easy sell or two. "Oh gosh, ma'am, I'm awful sorry to be pulling you away from your dinner."

"Oh, I don't mind. What's your bidness?"

"My name is Henry Dampier, and I'm proud to be of Christian service to you. I've got something very pretty in this little box here that I'd like to show you if you've got a minute or two, but I tell you what, ma'am — I'm going to sit right here on this porch until you finish your meal, and then I'll show you what I've got. I'm in no hurry at all."

"You come on in," she said. "It's mighty hot out here. We got a fan on inside."

"It's been hot up in North Carolina too, where I'm from. And dry. It got so dry my uncle ate three acres' worth of corn in one sitting."

"What's that?"

"It's hot and dry up in North Carolina."

"Come on in and get you a bite to eat and a glass of ice tea, if you're a mind." She pushed open the screen door all the way. "Pleased to meet you, Mr. . . . what was the name?"

"Henry Dampier."

"I'm Eloise Finley. Pleased to meet you."

"Pleased to meet you, Mrs. Finley." Henry stepped into the living room. "Mighty fine," he said. An oscillating fan, slowly facing one way, then the other, sat on a small table by an arched entryway to the dining room. Doilies and baby dolls in the living room. A picture on the wall of the collie protecting the sheep just like the one Aunt Dorie had. "We had that same picture when I was growing up. Something sure smells good."

"You ain't been growed up too long," said Mrs. Finley. "Let me have your hat."

"Thank you very much." He didn't see a Bible about.

In the dining room, a round wood dining table, a half-full plate sitting near a pulled-back chair, a few bowls of food on the table, and there: another woman, older, little, sitting quietly, chewing, looking at him.

"How do?" Henry nodded.

She nodded back. "Tolerable, thank you."

Mrs. Finley said, "That's my sister, Sarah."

"Howdy," said Sarah. "Sit down there."

Henry sat in the chair across from Miss Sarah. "Thank you. You remind me of my Aunt Sis, Mrs. Finley," he said to Mrs. Finley, now over at the stove. "Used to cook me cabbage. She cooked it with a spot of red pepper."

"I put a little red pepper in my cabbage. And collards too. I'll fix you a plate. Is there anything you don't like?"

"No ma'am. This is mighty nice. I do appreciate it." He smelled freshly cut cucumber — in vinegar? He eyed Mrs. Finley's plate: a full potato broken open with a fork, and it looked like a half a pork chop with gravy on it, a few string beans, and slices of cucumber and tomato. "Mighty nice," he said, looking around.

"Sarah had a stroke a while back," said Mrs. Finley from the stove, "but she's about got over it."

Sarah looked at him.

Mrs. Finley said, loudly, "Sarah, tell him about kissing Orvis."

"I didn't kiss my husband afore we was married and I didn't kiss him after."

"And tell him how many children you had," said Mrs. Finley.

"Eleven," she said with a big smile. She had two teeth down bottom, and that seemed to be about it.

"That's something," said Henry. "Eleven children."

"And I lost two besides that."

"I'm sorry."

"Sarah is ninety-one year old."

"Well, she don't look it." He thought: She looks ninety-eight.

"And she still drives her car out there too. But she won't eat like she ought to."

Sarah said, "You eat it."

"I don't want it. It's yourn."

"I don't want no more."

"I was just thinking about your health, Sarah. You've got to eat for stamina. Vitality. Right, Mr. Henry?"

"Yes ma'am."

"She fell in the garden last year, a few weeks before she had her stroke. We never could figure if there was any connection — you know, if there'd been two strokes. Anyway, she couldn't get up, and stayed out there two or three hours till we went looking for her late in the afternoon. We thought she'd walked down the road to our neighbor's garden for some peppers — we didn't grow any last year — and then when we found her right out back, there she lay in the corn rows, with her hands all dirty. Tell him, Sarah."

Sarah picked up her napkin, wiped her mouth, and said, "I weeded as far as I could reach."

Mrs. Finley placed a plate of food in front of Henry. She sat, closed her eyes, and Henry closed his. "Dear Lord," she said, "again, for these and the many blessings thou hast given us, we are eternally grateful. In our Saviour's blessed name, amen."

"Miss Sarah," said Henry, "you think you might could drive me up to Jeffries?"

She looked at him, chewed. Chewed some more. "It'll cost you."

"That's fine. How about a new Bible?"

"I could use a new Bible."

"Two Bibles," said Henry. "One for Mrs. Finley. Plus a tank of gas." Marleen, Marleen. Marleen Green.

"Sarah," said Mrs. Finley, "I don't think you —"

"Aw, I can drive to Jeffries and back," said Miss Sarah. "I did it while Orvis was alive. Many a time."

Henry thought, Well, that's a load off my mind.

"We'll talk about that later," said Mrs. Finley. "So it's Bibles you're selling?"

"Yes'm. Selling the word of the Lord. It's one of the most noble selling jobs I can imagine."

"It's all a paved road now," said Miss Sarah. "There and back."

"If it was paved there," said Mrs. Finley, "I'd think it'd be paved back." Then she said to Henry, "If she gets determined, there ain't no stopping her."

"There was that road to Atlanta," said Miss Sarah, "that stayed paved on just the going side for over two years — don't you remember that?"

"Oh, I see. That's right. Anyway, Mr. Henry, I guess we could drop you off in Jeffries and drive on into Atlanta. I'd like to go to the dime store."

"That would be fine with me," said Henry. "Yes ma'am."

"Let me go put on some lipstick," said Miss Sarah. "This dress is all right, don't you think?" she asked Mrs. Finley.

"It's fine, Sarah."

By the front door, on a little table, Henry noticed, was a framed photograph of a man in his coffin. "Who is that?" he asked.

"Oh, that's Orvis," said Mrs. Finley. "Sarah's husband."

It was a picture taken from the foot of the coffin, more or less, a proud old man in coat and tie, white flowers in the background. Henry looked around the room for another photograph of Orvis, then stood for a minute. "Do you-all have something a little younger?" he asked Mrs. Finley.

"Not handy," she said.

Henry, his valise in one hand, Miss Sarah's arm in his other, stepped slowly down the front steps. She was so tiny. She grasped the straps to her purse in one hand — the purse bumped a step on each step down — and the car keys in the other. Mrs. Finley, following, said, "She can't see all that good, but it'll be good for her to get out. She ain't drove in . . . I don't know how long it's been."

"Has she drove since she had her stroke?" asked Henry.

"Well . . . Sarah, have you drove since you had your stroke? I don't remember."

"What?"

"Have you drove since you had your stroke?"

"I don't think it was a stroke."

"That's what the doctor said."

"He won't all that smart, if you ask me. His secatery wouldn't even look at you." She halted, glared up at Henry. "I can't stand it when a body won't even look at you."

"Yes ma'am," said Henry. "Have you driven since you got sick?"

"I think I did. Let's get in the car."

"I'll be glad to drive," said Henry.

"That's a good idea," said Mrs. Finley. "Wait a minute. Let me go back and get my handbag. He's going to drive, Sarah."

Miss Sarah halted again, frowned. "He's going to what?"

"Drive," said Henry. "If that's okay with you."

"I don't think so. I want to drive. I like to drive. Where are we going?"

"Jeffries. Up to Jeffries."

Mrs. Finley, coming down the steps with her pocketbook, said, "She wants to drive, I bet."

Henry turned. "Yes ma'am."

"Then it's nothing much we can do. I'll sit in the back."

The car faced out of the garage. Henry opened the driver's door for Miss Sarah. Two bed pillows rested on her seat. She reached in and smoothed the top one. "Them pillowcases need changing," she said. She looked up at Henry. "Why you need to go to Jeffries?"

"To see my girlfriend," he said. He felt like spring had come.

"Oh. Well. That's a good reason." She slowly climbed into the seat. It took her a while. Henry closed the door. Mrs. Finley sat in back with her door closed.

Henry got in, noticed a radio on the dashboard. "Oh, good. You got a radio."

"I thought it would be a nice thing to have," said Mrs. Finley from the backseat.

Miss Sarah inserted the key, turned it, stepped on the starter; the engine turned for a few seconds and then caught. She stepped on the clutch, pulled the floor gear lever into first, and drove out the driveway and into the road, looking both ways but not stopping.

They were quiet for a few miles.

"I didn't even look at the gas," said Miss Sarah. "How much gas is in there? I can't read the dial."

Henry leaned over. "It's about half full." He felt a hope, an urgency, yeasting up. The ladies would drive off and leave him there with her. He could maybe get a kiss somehow and then the next time would be at night up at the motel, or somewhere, and . . . He'd kissed Amanda Dunn on two school hayrides in eighth grade, and then a few months later he'd kissed Gladys Fellpell — who everybody had kissed — coming home from the Fishertown skating rink in the bed of Mr. Dunn's pickup. Gladys had told him right after the kiss that she loved him, and he was so nervous he told her he loved her too. He didn't especially like her, though, because she wanted to talk all the time and had given him a skull ring that Aunt Dorie told him looked like it had something to do with the devil. After Gladys, Carson told him about Song of Solomon and the bra strap thing, and he'd had his three main girlfriends, Nan Faircloth, Dorothy Cox, and Betty Beal. And he'd discovered why Mrs. Long, the Latin teacher and counselor, told all the girls not to ever do heavy petting. It was because they got hot — and ready to do about anything, it looked like. But he'd saved himself. He'd promised Aunt Dorie.

After about an hour they passed the Night's Rest Motel. "We need to turn in right there at that fruit stand," he said. She'd made a new sign and changed the ECT. to ETC. He saw the scales — and Marleen under the tent all alone, exactly as he'd seen her over and over in his mind.

Marleen noticed the black car as it slowed, turned off the

road, and pulled up too close to the squash. It sat there running. An old woman, it looked like, or a child, was driving. Instead of the engine just quitting, the car lurched backward and choked to a stop. Somebody getting out on the passenger side and . . . was it . . . ? She stood. "Henry?" It *was* Henry. Who were the old ladies? He'd brought his grandmas? Or he'd hitchhiked?

She walked out from under the tent, extended her hand, palm down, and said, "Hey, Henry. I'm so glad you're back. I was hoping you might be."

"Hey, Marleen. These ladies are driving into Atlanta and they want to meet you." Marleen stood at the passenger window and Henry introduced them.

As they drove away, he said, "I was lucky to run up on them."

"The one driving looked pretty old."

"She was. Ninety-one."

"Come on under the tent. What happened the other day?"

He explained about being called away, about the cabin camp on the Okaloga near Brownlee, then listened as she told about waiting for him. She was sure something had gone wrong. She wasn't mad at all. She asked about the ladies. He told about his visit with them, that they were sisters, and about their stop at a service station and Miss Sarah thinking the man who pumped gas was one of her sons.

A car stopped, a family — man, woman, and two girls — got out, came in, and walked among the fruits and vegetables. They made their purchases and left, and Henry and Marleen talked again — this time about the family just there, guessing how old the two girls were, the man's job, where they were from. Henry forgot God, country, Bibles, and FBI work. Marleen forgot her sister, the chickens to kill, the bookmobile. The shape of Marleen's face, the texture of her voice, the laugh, her loveliness, all made themselves into a new form that Henry could almost feel with his hands, as real to him as the Jesus he'd once followed down the aisle at church. Already locked into Marleen's memory were Henry's long eyelashes, the unruly hair sticking up on the back of his head, the blood veins up from the arms, the long fingers, animated eyes, and his mother wit. She would write a poem about him.

They talked about aspirin and whether or not it actually stopped pain or covered it up. Henry said it just covered it up, that the pain was still there. Marleen said if you didn't feel the pain then the pain was not there, since pain can't happen until you feel it, even though the reason for the pain might be the very same as it was. Henry thought about it, said she was probably right.

Two men in dirty clothes drove up and bought two apples and a jar of jelly. They sat on the tailgate of their truck in the shade and ate. They'd brought along a loaf of bread, a jar of peanut butter, and a couple of Big Top grape drinks.

Henry thought about "have," "know," and "that." He explained how you sometimes couldn't for sure talk about an object in some ways unless you knew which particular one it was so that you could say *that* one. Marleen was confused at first, but then said that many times *she had thought just about the very same thing.* Yes, you couldn't make any real sense about certain kinds of tree things if you talked about trees in general. You needed to say *that* tree, and then talk about just one, where it was, where the first limb was, what had marked it up. Marleen had the concept down: "Sometimes generalizations don't work," she said.

Then Henry went to work on "have." He described the differences between a woman having a baby and having a car and having a headache, yet it was all the same word. You could get rid of a car in a minute, but not a headache. And to have a baby meant give birth to. Why give so much work to one little word?

The DeSoto pulled in — the ladies, back to get him. Henry stood slowly. Marleen stood beside him, leaned into him just enough so that their shoulders touched. He was suffering some now. He thought about Clearwater. They were supposed to meet that night, weren't they?

She put her arm behind him, tucked her thumb into the waist of his pants. He felt possessed by bright comfort. She stood on her tiptoes and kissed him on the cheek. He placed a hand on her neck and kissed her lips.

"Oh, Henry," she said, and placed her ear against his cheek.

He'd been run over by a moving mountain.

Back at Mrs. Finley's, Henry stood in the yard and talked to Mrs. Finley for a while. Miss Sarah had said she had to get ready for bed. They talked about the weather and gardens, and Mrs. Finley invited him to come back anytime.

Henry walked down to the cabin camps and met Clearwater driving out the long driveway. The hot afternoon sun had dropped into the tops of trees across a wide field. Clearwater's elbow was propped in the open window. "Sell any Bibles?"

"I sold a few. Won't we supposed to meet tonight?"

"That's tomorrow night. You couldn't remember?"

"Well, no. I was thinking —"

"I said tomorrow night. Get that fruit stand out of your head. You haven't been up there, have you?"

"No. Oh no. I been selling Bibles. Or trying to. Where you going?"

"I might drink a beer or two over at the truck stop, do some planning. See you later."

Henry walked to the bank of the river, sat on the wall. It was not the river it had been yesterday. It was a new river in a new world. His new thoughts and feelings spilled, stumbled, tumbled over each other. He wanted to take Marleen to McGarren Island, to the mountains, show her things. He remembered the old man, the fiddle player, at Indian Springs, up in the mountains, sitting by the spring every day for an hour, playing songs, talking to people who came for water. He'd said the two big invisible life ingredients were hope and fear, and that people took doses of hope from the springs in their jars and jugs and sheepskins. That was when Henry had first arrived up there to sell Bibles, and the fiddler told him all about the history of the springs — the little boy who found it and realized next day that his sore throat was cured by the water, about all the other people cured. He remembered that the fiddle player said he didn't believe in the water but believed in the hope that it made. He said fear was hope's brother, that both could do bad and good things to people, just like water and liquor. He'd said water could rot wood and revive plants, and that liquor could rot marriages and revive storytelling. He wore a hat with sweat stains, and his fiddle had a .22 bullet hole in it. Sleeping on a cot in the tool shed behind the Indian Springs Hotel was when Henry got cold and realized he'd come to the mountains too early in the spring, and on leaving, met Clearwater. If he hadn't met Clearwater, he realized, he wouldn't have met Marleen.

Clearwater had decided to take his little pearl-handled .32 pistol with him to the truck stop and bar they'd passed on the way into the cabin camp. The last time he was in a bar alone, he'd needed a pistol and didn't have it.

Six or eight tractor-trailers were parked in a large gravel lot near a service station with pumps out front for cars and pumps out back for trucks. Beyond the service station was a bar with a screened-in porch. A sign atop the bar said THE SUPPER CLUB. A larger sign out front, beside the highway, said OKALOGA TRUCK STOP AND RESTAURANT, and below that was another sign: ALL YOUR TRUCKING AND STOMACH NEEDS MET HERE.

The lighting was dim inside the bar. He found a seat at a small table and was approached by an aproned woman with red-and-gray hair. "What can I get for you, honey?" she asked.

"How about a can of Schlitz." It had been way too long. She was a little bit old. He would wait until they were up in Swan Island. They'd have those couple of days before picking up the truck and forklift. The boy had asked that they go up a few days early, and that was fine with him.

He'd brought his folder inside so he could study the plantation safe gig. There were maps and diagrams. Blinky was good about getting topographical maps to him. Clearwater marked a back road alternative, planned, and drank for over an hour. He checked his watch. He could stay and drink a fifth beer or head on home.

The waitress had disappeared on him, sort of, so he paid for his beers at the register and left through the door but returned and bought four to go.

He hadn't driven far when he realized that one of his front tires — felt like the right one — was flat. A wagon trail turned off to the right. He turned in and parked in a clear area far enough back in the woods not to be seen. He opened the trunk and got out the spare tire and rolled it around to the front right tire, which was sure enough flat. He went back to the trunk for the jack. It wasn't there. He'd never bothered to look — never imagined he'd need to bother to look. For the *jack?* What the hell? He'd just have to walk back there to that bar and get a jack, and he might as well steal one, because since he had the crowbar in the car, he could take that along and crack open a trunk with it. Any model jack would be okay. He could make it work. He'd mixed and matched before. He got a flashlight from the glove compartment.

He walked along the road back the way he'd come. Tall pines stood along both sides of the road. No cars coming either way. A bright moon, almost full, cast shadows.

He saw twinkles of truck-stop lights through the trees. He wondered if maybe the twinkles were blurry because of the beers he'd had. A car approached from ahead, and before it was close, he stepped over the road ditch, knelt, and dropped his head. He remembered the boy's story about his daddy. No reason to be seen at a time like this. As he squatted he could feel the pistol tight against his butt. He rested both hands on the crowbar as if it were a cane.

When he rounded the last curve he saw the six or eight tractor-trailer rigs in the large parking lot between him and the truck stop. On his side of the rigs sat a lone automobile. Chevrolet, a '48, it looked like. He stepped across the ditch and over a low wooden fence and walked up to the back of the car and stood there a minute. He placed the teeth of the crowbar into the lips of the trunk and pried once, got the teeth in further, and with a few quick jerks he had the trunk open. He stood for another moment, not moving, except for his eyes. Then he shined the light in the trunk and found the jack, got it, cut off the flashlight, stuck it in his pocket, eased the trunk lid down, and started back the way he'd come — cradling the jack and crowbar under his arm.

He heard a big rig truck door open, the closest one. Somebody yelled "Hey," and he heard a cab door slam. How could that be? He should have checked the cab, should have looked in, knocked on the door. Stupid mistake. Somebody had been asleep in there. He kept walking at a steady pace. The man called "Hey" again. Clearwater didn't look back. He switched the jack and crowbar from under his right arm to under his left, reached into his back pocket, pulled out the pistol and held it at his belt buckle. It was ready to fire — a bullet already jacked into the chamber. He just wanted to change a tire. Most other cars he'd have left behind. He heard the man running up behind him, breathing hard. He didn't want any interference — couldn't afford any. The man had made a huge mistake. Clearwater stopped, then turned around, the pistol just out of sight behind his leg.

"Where the hell you think you're going with that?" said the man, glaring in the light of the moon. He grabbed the jack and jerked it to his side, knocking the crowbar to the ground, slapped Clearwater across the face. "You asshole," the man said.

He's not even aware of the crowbar, thought Clearwater. His face stung. Without speaking, he shot the man in the stomach. The man grunted, grabbed his stomach, then turned and faced the other way, his feet still planted as they had been, as if he couldn't start his retreat. Clearwater shot him in the back of the head. He dropped. Clearwater's upper lip was numb and his chin felt all tingly, not from the slap, but from what he'd just done. The man was facedown and moving a little, but he wouldn't be moving long, Clearwater figured. He felt for the man's billfold in the back left pocket, then back right pocket, where he found it. It was thick. He slid it down into his right front pocket. He looked all around to be sure nobody had seen.

He picked up the jack and trotted down the road until he was sure he was out of the line of sight from the truck stop. There was a good chance the trucks had blocked the sound of the pistol shots from the bar. It was just the little .32. He walked down the wagon path to the Chrysler. He was glad he'd thought to park off the main road. He set up the jack and changed the tire. His hands were shaking a little. He'd wait awhile, get the old tire fixed, and buy a new jack, maybe from a Chrysler dealer. Sometimes the police got lucky in putting two and two together. You couldn't be too cautious.

He didn't like to shoot people, but sometimes it just happened because it was the only way to get through some problem to a place where he had to be. No other way to handle it. Nobody should ever slap anybody like that.

Henry was awake when Clearwater drove into the cabin camp. He pulled back his window shade and looked. Clearwater opened his trunk, lifted something out — a crowbar? a car jack? — and walked into the woods with it. What was he doing? He lay back down, thought of Marleen, her blond hair, the way it hung around her face.

Back in his room, Clearwater sat on his bed. Leaving before they were scheduled to leave might look suspicious. No need to run. No way to trace the mess to him. No way at all.

*   *   *

A drawbridge for automobiles, rather than a single trolley track, now spanned the channel from McNeill to Swan Island. Henry — in the driver's seat — and Clearwater waited for the drawbridge to lower. As he had driven the Chrysler north from South Carolina, where they'd been working for over a week, Henry told Clearwater about his memories of the trolley, the Electra, the lights, the band, and what he'd heard from his aunt about his uncle's plan that night long ago. How it had gone bad. Clearwater knew of the Electra and the big bands, of good fishing, of German sub sightings from the island, and had decided to come up a couple of days early — like Henry asked — before picking up the dump truck and forklift for their next gig, in Florida.

A yacht was moving through the drawbridge gap. Low white clouds scatted along the sky, and a clean salt smell rode the air through the open car windows.

"That's something, ain't it?" said Clearwater. "You could live in a yacht and never come out except for some fun. Hire some people to do everything for you."

As they turned right at the big Papa John McNeill mansion on Swan Island, Henry decided he'd better tell Clearwater about Caroline, Carson, and Aunt Dorie. He'd made arrangements, had reserved three rooms at the Deluxe Olympia Hotel, a place Carson told him about on the telephone. It was close to the Electra. A room for Clearwater, a room for Caroline and Aunt Dorie, and a room for him and Carson. But Clearwater didn't know about all that.

"Some of my folks might be down here," said Henry.

"What?"

"My sister and cousin and aunt. The ones I've told you about."

"What do you mean 'they might be down here'?"

"I sort of mentioned to them that I was going to be here, and . . . But I didn't say anything about you."

"Why the hell didn't you check with me? This is not a good idea at all. Goddamn, Dampier."

"But we're not working."

"What have you told them about me?"

"Nothing. I just wanted to see them a little bit — and you didn't want to go through Simmons. So I just kind of set things up. Told them I could get them a room and all. They don't have to know anything about you. I started not to tell you at all — just . . . I knew you'd be in a different room and —"

"You can't hide information from me. This is serious business." Clearwater felt something slip away from him. But he'd be through with Henry within a couple of weeks. "You go ahead and check in and then I will. I'll take the car, and I'll see you Monday morning in front of the hotel. Seven thirty. I'm going to do a little scouting around."

"There's the Electra right down there. See it? I think that's it. The hotel is just beyond it. Yeah, that's it."

Henry slowed the car and in a minute stood, holding his suitcase and valise. He could identify the building by its shape — in spite of its having been converted into three distinct places of business: Swan Island Laundry and Dry Cleaning, Bobbins Hardware, and Dance Hall Bar. The hardware store, the one in the middle, looked closed down. A mattress lay on its steps. Plants grew from the gutters.

Henry walked through the front doorway of the lobby at the Deluxe, carrying his valise and suitcase. The back door was open to the ocean. Caroline sat on a couch reading a magazine. She looked up. He set down his suitcase and valise.

"Henry! Hey," she said. She stood, moved to him. "We've been missing you." She wrapped her arms around his neck and pulled him tight.

He hugged her. "I wish I could have come to Simmons, but this ought to be fun."

"I know. The beach! Sit down for a minute."

"Did you see the Electra?" asked Henry.

"It's terrible. It looks run-down."

"I never thought about it changing."

"Me either."

Henry sat in a big chair. He looked around. "This looks like a nice place. Where's Carson?"

"He's swimming and wants you to come out. Thank you for our room. You didn't have to do that. We could have stayed over in McNeill."

"No. I'm glad I can do this. I figured this would be a good time to catch up on things. I've got another couple of weeks of pretty regular work, and then I'll have some time to come home, I think. Let's go swimming."

"Sure. I've got to put on my bathing suit. Come on up."

"Is Aunt Dorie on the beach?"

"She couldn't come. She stepped on a nail this morning, out behind the packing barn. That tall grass out there. But she wants you to come see her if you can. Do you have a car? I never quite figured that out."

"I do and I don't. It's kind of complicated. I'll be able to tell you before too long what I'm doing."

"It's not dangerous — or crazy — is it?"

"Oh no. Not a bit. Did you drive?"

"Carson drove. He could take you to see Aunt Dorie tomorrow, maybe. Up and back."

A short while later, as Clearwater checked in at the desk, he heard Henry talking, coming downstairs into the lobby. He saw him, and . . . and . . . a stunning woman. In her neck and shoulders and face he recognized a proud vulnerability and loveliness that almost called aloud to him. The boy's *sister?* In a bathing suit, a big white towel around her waist. He stood staring.

Caroline noticed the man standing at the registration counter. And then, just as she entered the doorway that led to the beach, she glanced back.

Clearwater walked over to the door, watched her walk, the light blue sky meeting the darker blue ocean far out ahead of her. He breathed in the clean salt breeze. Another boy, the cousin probably, ran up to Henry and they started talking and laughing. She let the towel *drop* and ran with the boys toward the ocean.

Carson and Henry decided to drive up to Simmons right away, see Aunt Dorie, and drive back before bedtime. That way they could then stay for two uninterrupted days at Swan Island. Caroline came out of the water, and as Henry and Carson walked across the sand toward her, they met Clearwater. Henry knew to pretend he didn't know him, but Clearwater raised his finger, stepped aside, said, "Give me just a minute."

Carson walked on ahead while Clearwater told Henry he'd changed his mind, there was a better way to proceed under the circumstances, a better way to handle things than trying to avoid each other — especially since they wouldn't be on call. They could say they were doing secret army work — USAUO, U.S. Army Undercover Operations — related to Russian spies, a problem with Russian submarines hanging around the island. He had some friends working on exactly that. He would handle it all.

"Can we tell them it's the FBI?" asked Henry.

"No. The procedure in a case like this is to say something like I just said, and that's it. You haven't told them anything, have you?"

"No. Nothing."

"Because if you have, this will get really confusing."

"I haven't told them anything."

"The less said, the better. Introduce us, let me talk, and then we can all relax."

Caroline, sitting on the quilt she'd brought from home, saw Henry, Carson, and the man approaching. She pulled the towel over her legs. The man wore pleated pants, suspenders, a blue tie and white shirt. He reminded her of somebody, but she couldn't place who. Clark Gable?

Where the gearshift came up out of the floorboard of the black '39 Plymouth was a hole that you could see through. Carson drove and Henry sat in the passenger seat. SIMMONS PRINTING, SIMMONS, N.C., 4-0948 was printed on the front door. The car belonged to Carson's boss. In the backseat sat two cardboard boxes holding seven hundred bumper stickers.

"Why can't you talk about it?" asked Carson.

"I just can't. I just can't. Before too long I can, probably. In a couple of weeks. It's a *lot* of stuff, boy. It —"

"That guy looked pretty neat, and it must be good money — you staying in a hotel and all. Do you and him use a gun or anything?"

"Not yet. I mean, I probably could, though. I can't talk about it now. Tell me some more about these bumper stamps."

"Bumper *stickers*. Oh man. I read a article about them, no wires for hanging, no nothing. Just wet the back and stick it on." Carson drove with one hand, talked with the other, looked back and forth between Henry and the road. "So I called this guy in Virginia, and he could send them to me for two cents each with nothing on them, and man they do stick good. Wet it with a wet rag. So I figured it'd be just the thing for the printing shop, and Mr. Ferguson says, okay, if I wanted to take it on — he wouldn't have time to mess with it — and I was thinking about sports teams, you know, stuff like that, and I was thinking *one for every car in North Carolina,* then in the South, then *in America,* okay, so I ordered this waterproof ink — a lot of people wouldn't have thought about the waterproof — from this place that had a special deal. I got red and black, and I figured out how to run it on the press, just practiced with cutout paper, same size, and then I got to thinking about what I could print on there, you know, where I could sell a lot of them, and all that, and I was thinking about a bunch of ball teams, maybe State, Carolina, Wake Forest, East Carolina, places like Ballard, all the minor league baseball teams, Little League, you know, figure out a way to get the mascot drawed on there — there's ways to do that — and some more colleges, and so then we got your call and I asked Mr. Ferguson for a vacation day, and I figured why not hurry up so I could sell them on the way to Swan Island, and maybe while I was down here too, so I just out of the blue thought about 'Jesus Saves,' and then I thought 'God Is My Co-Pilot' and then 'Where Will You Spend Eternity?'"

Henry was thinking about Marleen, calling her on the phone.

"So, see, I'm not talking about every car in America exactly, but I'm talking about every *Christian* car in America, and that's a lot of cars, and so what I did on the way down is I sold them for five cents each at these stores, service stations, grocery stores, and a couple of stores bought *fifty,* and I'm selling them for five cents each, and then I'll come back to the store in a month to pick up the ones they ain't sold — that they don't want to keep — I buy them back and for the ones that are already sold or ones they know they want to keep I collect five *more* cents, see — I got it all wrote down — and then they get to sell them for whatever they want to, I said fifteen cents, so they make five cents each, and I figure ten cents is wholesale, and if they don't want some I give them back a nickel apiece, but I've only got that two cents for the blank bumper sticker in it *up front,* plus the ink, which ain't nothing, and then, so I'll make at least seven cents on each one, so those seven hundred in the backseat, hell, man, that's forty-nine dollars clear profit, and I haven't even *tried.* I haven't even *tried.*"

Henry had the phone number on a piece of paper in his billfold.

"That's selling at wholesale, and I could sell them retail and make twenty-five more dollars on that first forty-nine. I've already called the guy up and ordered a thousand more and on Monday I might order more. And listen, they go like hotcakes, I'm telling you. And my phone number is right there on the bumper sticker, and my business name, so when I get back home I bet you I'll be getting orders — it says 'Carson's Premier Printing, Simmons, N.C., phone 6-5912' and all. It's not like just anybody can do this, not everybody has a printing press — and so heck, man, I'm starting my own company. Trucks, sooner or later, shipments, orders. So I got to thinking on the way down here. If I order two thousand, that's forty dollars my cost, okay, and then I could find forty churches. I know I could find forty churches. And you know they'd buy fifty each. I'll tell them just put one in each hymnbook. That ought to work. Sell them at ten cents each and that's two hundred dollars total —"

"You sure you got the math right?"

"I got the math right. I figured it. What you've got then is, see, one dollar per church I'm spending and I'm making *five*. So what *you* could do if you want to go in with me is you buy five thousand and I buy five thousand and you don't have to do nothing. You spend a hundred dollars, and what I'll do when I sell one of your bumper stickers is I keep five cents and you keep five cents, and so you're making good — you'll get back two hundred and fifty dollars for every hundred dollars you spend, and what I'll get is two fifty for being out on the road selling them along with mine. You don't lift a finger. What do you think?"

"Sure. Here." Henry got out his billfold, handed two twenties to Carson. "I can get the rest back at the hotel," he said. He looked to be sure the phone number was in its place.

"Damn. You are making some money."

"And listen. I got a fruit stand I can get some sold at maybe. I got to tell you about that."

"Where?"

"Down in Jeffries, Georgia."

"You bought a fruit stand?"

"No. No, it's just one I know about — where I met this girl."

"Yeah? Fruit stands, grocery stores will be good places to

sell. Watch this. This Gulf station coming up. I'll pull in. Where's Jeffries? What about the girl?"

"Not far from Atlanta. There's this girl that runs the fruit stand, and I'm definitely going back to see her first chance I get. I got this ride to see her with these two old ladies, and I'm supposed to call her tonight. She don't have a phone, but her sister does, where she'll be. Her name's Marleen Green. Marleen. Marleen. Marleen Green."

"Yeah, take her a bunch of bumper stickers. I want to hear about it, but wait, just watch this. We stopped at nine stores on the way down here — I just stopped at ones on the right side of the road 'cause I knew we didn't have time to stop at them all. That way I could remember. It added some time to the trip, but we sold three hundred bumper stickers easy as *pie*. That's thirty dollars in one day, not even trying. Do you realize that that's over ten thousand dollars in one year? Ten thousand dollars, on bumper stickers? Let's see — thirty, thirty, nine hundred, nine thousand, two times nine hundred, eighteen hundred. That's ten thousand eight hundred dollars in one year."

They pulled into a service station, the parking area covered with rocks and bottle caps.

"But it'll have to be more than just driving back and forth to the beach," said Henry, "and you're not going to sell any on Sundays, and you just might have got lucky here at first. Beginner's luck. Selling Bibles, I can tell you, it really comes and goes. Oh, I've got to tell you about this cat with a tooth stuck through a copperhead's head."

They were inside the Gulf station.

"Wait a minute," whispered Carson. "Watch."

The store owner, a man with his arm in a sling, bought forty bumper stickers. Twenty JESUS SAVES, and ten each of the other two.

Back in the car and on the road, Carson said, "That's the way it is everywhere. Now, what about this woman?"

Henry told Carson about Marleen.

Carson wanted to know if he got into her pants.

Henry told him no, but that he probably would before long.

"*What?* You probably *will?*"

"I don't know. I've changed my ideas about a lot of things."

"What happened?"

"I started reading the Bible."

When they arrived at the homeplace, Aunt Dorie sat waiting on the front doorstep. She stood slowly, a big smile on her face. As Henry walked toward her, she said, "I'd run to meet you if it won't for my foot." They hugged, and she sat and patted the step beside her. Henry sat. Carson parked himself in a metal lawn chair close by. Dorie held Henry's hand in her lap. "I want you to tell me what-all you been doing. It must be pretty fine, and Carson, you're going to have to do something about the phone. It's been ringing off the hook. People wanting more of them bumper stickers. There it goes right now."

Carson jumped up. "This is something like wildfire," he said.

"Where's Uncle Samuel?" Henry asked Aunt Dorie.

"He's in Raleigh. He'll be back before supper. He's so good to me, Henry."

"I'm glad."

Caroline sat and talked with this older friend of her brother's about the Grand Ole Opry, about Roy Acuff, whom he knew, Red Foley, whom he'd met, about schoolteaching, which Caroline was doing, first grade, about his first school principal, his armed service experience in France, about Russia getting an atomic bomb, the possibility of war in Korea, and about losing a child, before he lost his wife. He seemed kind and asked her question after question about her teaching, and while he asked, it came to her that Glenn never asked those kinds of questions. It also came to her that he looked like Clark Gable, for sure. Henry had mentioned him in his letters, but not how handsome he was. He seemed like a man who had been places, but was also kind and thoughtful. They got to talking about their favorite songs and he, off-key, sang a few lines of "Sentimental Journey." They both laughed. Glenn loved her in his own way, but he'd yet to say "I love you." His word was "care." He'd been needy and eager in a sexual way, and she finally gave in. Though she knew it was wrong, it was somehow difficult to back out of it, avoid it — Glenn was unpleasant when she tried to talk about waiting. And how in the world had it turned out that she was sitting on the beach with this kind man who was talking to her, the sun going down, time suspended? Where were the boys?

When she got back to her room — Preston had offered to take her to dinner, and there was no reason to say no — there was a note on the door. Carson had called and would call back.

During supper with Carson, Aunt Dorie, and Uncle Samuel, Henry explained what little he could about his secret job. He wished Uncle Jack were there.

He talked a lot about Bible selling, the lessons he'd learned from Mr. Fletcher, and how they'd panned out. He told the cat-snake story. He talked about Indian Springs, the hotel there, the fiddle player, how people visited from all over.

He got the latest news about Aunt Ruth, Uncle Delbert, others in the family. And Aunt Dorie made him promise he'd come home for a while as soon as possible.

While they sat around the table after the meal, Uncle Samuel asked Henry what was the most important thing he'd learned in the last few months.

"It looks like I learned today to get in the bumper sticker business."

"Well, I guess as long as it's Christian bumper stickers," said Uncle Samuel. "Yep, it looks like he might be onto something."

Henry imagined Uncle Jack talking about bumper stickers — his chin tucked into his neck, the way he would sit back on the back two legs of his chair.

"Have you-all been down to Swan Island anytime lately?" Henry asked Uncle Samuel and Aunt Dorie.

They hadn't.

"The Electra that used to be so nice is plumb run-down," he said. He wanted to remember aloud about the time they went with Uncle Jack, but knew not to.

"I think," said Carson, "if we wait to go back till tomorrow morning we could stop at some churches. Some of the big ones that might have an office or a preacher house next door."

"Parsonage," said Aunt Dorie, and then to Henry, "Did you get to spend any time with Caroline?"

"Just a few minutes. Mr. Clearwater, the man I was telling you about, was talking to her when we left."

"Oh. How old is Mr. Clearwater?" said Aunt Dorie.

"I don't know. Maybe forty. What would you say, Carson?"

"Something like that. Pretty old."

"He was in the war," said Henry. Then he understood. "Oh no, he's way too old for her. And somehow I don't think he's all that interested in women. I mean, I don't mean he's a fairy or anything, but he just . . . I think he had a wife and a bad marriage a long time ago, something like that. I didn't get to ask Caroline about Glenn. Are they still going out?"

"I think Glenn will come to his senses and ask her to marry him before the summer's over," said Uncle Samuel. "I've more or less pushed him to make a move before he gets too ugly to marry." He laughed and looked around. "And I've helped him out with his business school."

"I guess they're almost engaged," said Aunt Dorie. "Shouldn't you-all try again to call her? We're all through eating, it looks like."

Carson phoned the hotel, asked for Caroline, and after a minute, talked to her, told her that over half the stores they'd stopped at on the way down had called to say they wanted more bumper stickers. They could make some quick money by waiting until the next morning to come back and take care of all the reorders.

She said that that would be fine, that she might take a walk on the beach, for them not to worry, and not to speed on the way down in the morning.

Then Henry called Marleen's sister's phone. This was the night. Friday. Between nine and ten. Marleen's sister, Tina, answered. A baby was crying. She was expecting his call and talked to him a minute — the boy she'd "heard so much about." Marleen came to the phone, and Henry, just inside the closed pantry door for privacy, felt the pantry become a kind of hallowed place. He looked at a row of canned tomatoes, one jar at a time, the "Ball" imprint standing out, the jars reflecting the lightbulb in the pantry ceiling. He listened to news, told his, and waited through one or two awkward silent spells. He told her about Swan Island, the bad condition of the Electra, the mattress on the steps. She told him about her grandma's fall, her daddy's hernia.

"I'll call you next Friday, same time, same place," he said.

"But I'll probably be at a coin phone, with a lot of nickels and dimes. You'll be there, right?"

"I'll be here," said Marleen.

"Well . . ." Maybe she would say something that could kind of get them started to saying good-bye. "Bye until next week, then," he said.

"Good-bye. Be sure to call me, now."

"Bye. I will."

"Bye."

". . . Bye."

". . . Good-bye . . ."

Before they went to bed Henry and Carson played carom and listened to *The Country Squire Show* on the radio, then Henry looked on the back table in the garage and found his cast net. In their bedroom after lights-out he and Carson talked about Korea. Carson said if a war happened it probably wouldn't last long because America had atom bombs and the North Koreans and Chinese didn't.

Caroline told Preston about her visit to the Electra when she was fourteen, about Aunt Dorie not wanting to dance. About the moon — and telling about that moon helped usher a kind of sea smoke into her heart, just as he, with his fingers, started at her wrist and continued on down toward her fingertips, a gentle, soft touching, and she, involuntarily almost, reached to the tie at his chest, grasped it, and as he kissed her, she moved her hand down the length of it — as if

holding her fingers around the stems of flowers — feeling
and hearing a voice say that all this had been ordained before
stars were born.

On Monday morning, Henry said good-bye to Carson and
Caroline — she acted funny the whole time they were at the
beach. Then at Johnson and Ball Construction and Industrial Machine Repair Company over in McNeill, the place
Blinky ran, or pretended to run, Henry learned to drive and
manage a forklift and a dump truck. A man named Skinny,
with orange-framed glasses, was his teacher. The FBI had
connections that he'd never dreamed of.

Just over the first bridge outside McNeill was a turnoff
onto a narrow dirt road that crossed a small bridge over a
creek. The creek appeared to run from the channel to a large
pond. Henry had a notion. He turned the big lumbering
dump truck onto the side road and stopped. Clearwater
pulled in behind him. Carson had stuck a "Jesus Saves" bumper sticker on the front bumper of the Chrysler and said he
was going to order ten thousand more.

Henry reached for his cast net in a bucket in the floorboard
and climbed down from the cab. He walked to Clearwater's
car window. "Get out. I want to show you something."

"What?"

"How to throw a cast net. You can show me how to light
a match in a thirty-knot wind. Mr. Blinky never did. Remember?"

"We need to get on the road."

"That gig's not till next Sunday. We got all kinds of time."

"Something might come up."

"Aw, come on."

Clearwater got out, and Henry walked him over to the bridge, then down an embankment, until they stood beside the creek.

"Okay," said Henry. "You take in the cord like this, shake it so all the weights are clear, and then catch it at about one-third of the way down and pick up a weight from down here, hold it here, and then get you another weight and spread out the net, and you're ready to go, see, and then you just stare out there for a little ripple that says 'finger mullet,' and if you don't see one you can throw blind. You've got to spin your right hand when you fling it, and so you go like this." Henry flung the net and it opened into a circle, landed, sank into the water. He started pulling in, hand over hand. As the bunched net got close he saw the silver minnow sides flashing, reflecting sky light. He thought of the disciples. "Okay, okay, we got a few. See. That was easy. Pull it up and then just grab this here to unpucker it in the bucket, like this, shake it, pull it up, and the fish fall out. You want to try it?"

Clearwater didn't know what to do. He took the net. He cast a few times, with Henry talking him through the process. No luck.

They started up the bank to the bridge.

"Now you got to teach me that match-lighting trick," said Henry. "Thirty-knot wind."

Clearwater took a deep breath. He reached into his shirt pocket for a box of matches. The morning sun was just coming from behind clouds.

"Okay. Put the match between your first and second finger, like this. Then you strike it, see? Like that, and cup your hand, and bring your other hand in so no air comes up from below or from either side. See?"

"Yessir."

"Blinky says it works in a wind up to thirty knots. Try it a few times without striking it. That's what he makes people do. . . . Okay. Good. Almost. Good. Now, see, you got to get your other hand in there — the heel of your other hand right up against here. . . . There you go. Good. Good. Now try striking one."

Henry lit the match, curved his fingers around the flame, brought in his other hand, cradling, like he might cradle a lightning bug.

Late that evening the dump truck, Chrysler following, passed houses whose interior lights, yellow through shades, or white through windows, had just come on or were coming on. Clearwater thought about having Caroline inside one of those houses, in the living room maybe, just kind of knocking things around. All that hard breathing, coming on so quick. She'd never once mentioned the name Glenn, from the very beginning, the one Henry said was her boyfriend. Available ones never mentioned husband or sweetheart names. Unavailable ones did. He would look her up again sometime — even a good ways down the line.

Just outside Jemson, Georgia, it started raining, a slow drizzle. Henry sighted a service station with a shelter and pulled in for gas and a drink. As he stepped around the back of the dump truck, he glanced at the front bumper of the Chrysler, stopped, gasped, closed his eyes, not wanting to believe, opened them again to see the tiny red and black rivers of ink and rainwater running down and off the bumper sticker and onto the chrome bumper, very little left of JESUS SAVES. But holding on at the bottom in small, proud print: "Carson's Premier Printing, Simmons, N.C., phone 6-5912."

PART IV

———

GENESIS

1938

———

A drop of water from Uncle Jack's finger fizzed in the frying pan. "Put on your coat and hat," he said to Henry, "and bring me in a bucket of stove wood." He turned the bacon slices with a fork, one at a time. Grease bubbled beneath them. Outside, darkness was dissolving into gray light.

Henry brought in the wood, dumped it into the wood box, took off his coat and hat, and sat at the breakfast table.

Uncle Jack turned bacon again, sang-talked: "Jack Sprat could eat no fat, his wife could eat no lean; and so between the two of them, they licked the platter clean." He lifted bacon slices on the fork and placed them on a clean rag. "Doodle-lee, doodle-lee, doodle-lee do. Doodle-lee, doodle-lee do."

He cracked an egg on the rim of the frying pan and opened the egg with one hand, dropped the yolk and white into the grease popping and sizzling, then cracked another, then another, tossing each shell into the trash can beside the woodstove. "Come here a minute. Here. Stand on . . . stand on this stool. Now. Look." Henry looked at the red tip of the match that was in his uncle's mouth. "Here's how you do this egg with one hand . . . Try it. No. You better use two. Like this . . . Okay. And if you don't have the pan real hot, the eggs'll stick. Here you go . . . Good job. Good job. That's kind of messy, but it ain't bad. Now sit back down over there."

Uncle Jack sang again. "They licked that platter left and right, they licked it up and down. They licked that platter front and back, they licked it all around. Doodle-lee, doodle-lee, doodle-lee do. Doodle-lee, doodle-lee do. Then one day while they did lick, their two tongues they did touch, and now old Jack's not worth two cents, he loves to kiss so much."

Jack set a plate in front of Henry.

Henry looked at the eggs. They had black bacon specks in them. When Uncle Jack started eating, he would mix his eggs and grits together with knife and fork.

Dorie came in.

"Do you want me to fix you a plate?" said Jack. "I got enough."

"I can fix it. And I'll make some sandwiches. I know you-all want to get on the road. Let's say the blessing." She looked to be sure that Henry was closing his eyes. He closed them.

"Dear Lord, please bless this food to the nourishment of our bodies, and to thy glory. In thy blessed name, amen."

Henry broke off the end of a crisp bacon strip. He touched his toast to the egg yellow near the grits.

Uncle Jack shook Texas Pete hot sauce from the bottle onto his eggs. "Want some of this?" he said.

"No sir."

They motored the boat out of the creek and into the calm sound, then along the shore until they came to another inlet. By this time light had moved into the air as if gaining confidence. In the east, above the coming sun, the sky was a muddy red. "We'll cut the motor and drift," said Uncle Jack. "Dip me a half bucket of water."

Henry made his way to the bucket, dropped it over the side. He played around with the lip of the bucket touching the water.

"Hurry up."

Uncle Jack gathered up the cast net and shook the weights loose from each other, stood on the bow. He held the net in one hand like a loose skirt gathered at the hips, a single lead weight under his thumb, a single weight in the other hand, and looked out across the water as they drifted.

Henry knew to look for a water ripple, but there were always water ripples, and he had a hard time telling the right ripples. Suddenly Uncle Jack swung the net back and then forward into a wide circle that splashed into the water, sinking quickly. He began pulling it in, hand over hand. "Ah, we got us a good mess," he said. Henry saw the picture of Jesus asking the disciples to throw the net on the other side of the boat. They did and caught fish. He leaned forward so he could see the flashing silver sides of the finger mullet underwater. Uncle Jack lifted the net over the bucket, shook and unpuckered it so that the small baitfish fell loose. Henry, leaning in with his hands on the cross plank so that he could see, watched them dart from side to side of the bucket and around the walls.

"Okay, now," said Uncle Jack, "let's motor up and drift along that marsh over there." He sat by the engine, wrapped the starter rope and pulled once, wrapped again and pulled, and the engine sputtered to life. He killed the motor when they were a good casting distance from shore so that they could drift along the marsh grass line and cast for red drum. Three rods and reels rested against the gunnels. "All right," said Uncle Jack, "get you a baitfish."

Henry reached into the cold water, chased, and closed his hand around a finger mullet. He positioned it in his left hand so that the head was visible. The boat quietly drifted. He held the hook in his right hand and placed its point on the finger mullet's eyeball and pushed so that the hook went through and pushed against the other eye from the inside, then came out. Henry could feel bone sockets move somehow.

"Good work," said Uncle Jack.

They fished without luck until midmorning.

"Let's wind 'em in, eat us these sam'iches," said Uncle

Jack. "Yum, yum." He dropped anchor, stood, moved to the front of the boat, then pulled a paper sack from the bow space, opened it, and got out two sandwiches wrapped in wax paper and a canteen of water. He looked out across the marsh and then up the inlet to the sound. The wind had risen since morning and there were waves, though no white-tops. He took in the sky all around. "Don't look like we'll be getting any rain." He took a bite of the sandwich. "Ummmm, good old monkey meat."

"Yes sir." Henry ate, drank a swig of water. He hadn't realized he was so thirsty. He felt enclosed in the refuge of the fishing trip, the rules, the boundaries: the placement weights, hooks, the operation of the reel, the net casting that only Uncle Jack could do, the waiting, the wallowing of the boat when someone stood and moved around, the need to stay close to center, the changing of water to keep the bait alive.

Uncle Jack moved the cork on the fishing line so that the finger mullet would be deeper. He cast, handed the rod to Henry. "Watch that cork, now. You can cast next time."

Henry's cork dropped out of sight. "I got one!"

"Whoa. Set the hook. Yank it."

Henry gave a pull and the line resisted solidly. His heart thumped in his neck. The rod tip dipped toward the water.

"That's right. Hold the tip up. Hold the tip up."

The fish swam in a big half circle, rising to ripple the water, then diving, the line leaving a moving V on the surface.

"Just hold on. Let him get tired. Reel in like I showed you."

Henry pulled the rod tip up high, then eased the pressure while winding, pulled up. Suddenly the fish started away — toward shallow water. The drag whined.

"He's a big one," said Uncle Jack. "You're playing him just right. Keep that tip up in the air." The drag whined again.

As the fish tired, Henry wound him in toward the boat. Uncle Jack found the landing net, knelt against the side of the boat, waited with a hand cradling the taut line. He scooped with the net and swung the shining drum, bronze-colored along the back, white on the belly, up into the boat. "It don't get no better than that, does it, boy?"

"No sir."

"It don't get no better. Now, you cast this time."

Henry cast. It was a good one.

By noon they'd caught eight redfish. "Let's go get some more lunch at Duke's," said Uncle Jack.

In the truck, riding along, Henry asked Uncle Jack about a dog dead on the road — if dogs ever had funerals.

"I don't think so. But some of them might. We'll give Trixie a funeral. We gave her mama and daddy one."

They sat in a booth at Duke's Bait and Burgers, eating a hamburger each. Jack ordered a Blatz beer and then another. "Don't you want some dessert?" he asked.

"Yes sir."

"What you want?"

"A piece of apple pie."

"Donna. Bring this boy a piece of apple pie." He took a long swig of beer. "Don't you want a cup of ice cream?"

"Yes sir."

Uncle Jack went to a freezer, pushed the top doors back, got a cup of vanilla ice cream and then a flat wooden spoon from a big glass jar. He sat and placed the cup and spoon in front of Henry, then pulled out a pouch of Prince Albert, some papers, and began to roll a cigarette. "Can you get that top off, bud?"

"Yes sir." Henry pulled on the little tab on the lid of the ice-cream cup.

Donna brought the pie.

"I'm going to have me one more Blatz to go with my cigarette," said Uncle Jack. He pulled a box of matches from his shirt pocket and lit the cigarette, shook out the match. He opened his billfold, held it open, toward Henry. "Pull me out that five-dollar bill. And a one."

Henry pulled them out, handed them to Uncle Jack, who motioned for Donna.

"What can I do for you?" she asked.

"I'll get one for the road." The cigarette stayed in place in Uncle Jack's lips.

"Yes sir."

"Donna, this is my brother-in-law's boy. You knew that, didn't you?"

She was headed back to the bar; she stopped, turned. "Oh yeah. Danny's boy."

Outside, Uncle Jack asked Henry to stand by the truck and wait for him. He crossed the street and entered the barbershop. Ten minutes later he came out with a leather jacket over his arm. Henry had never seen it. In the truck on the ride home, Henry looked at the jacket, on the seat between them, several times. Uncle Jack explained. "It's just something I *acquired*. It ain't something you need to mention to Aunt Dorie or anybody else. Okay?"

"Yes sir."

When Uncle Jack pulled the truck into the driveway and up beside the house, Aunt Dorie came out to meet them. She stopped and didn't move toward them. She watched Uncle Jack unhitch the boat with some difficulty. Then she walked up and looked in the truck cab.

"What?" he said. "Wha's a matter?"

Aunt Dorie ordered Henry inside.

After a while, when Aunt Dorie came in, Henry asked her where Uncle Jack was.

"He's checking his rabbit boxes."

Henry watched from the back window, looking down the wagon path that came out of the woods, the path lit by the garage light. Uncle Jack came bouncing along, carrying two rabbits by their hind legs. "He's back!" Henry said to Aunt Dorie. "Can I go out there?"

"Go ahead."

In the backyard, at the cleaning table, Henry watched as Uncle Jack with his pocketknife punched into a rabbit's skin on its back, then cut where a belt would be. Its eyes were open and cloudy. Henry would sometimes talk to a dead rabbit when Uncle Jack left to go to the smokehouse for the hatchet. He'd say, "Hey there, little rabbit."

"Okay," said Uncle Jack. A cigarillo hung from his lips. He puffed, chewed tobacco. "You pull his pants off, and I'll get his shirt. That's right. Pull hard, boy. Now, good. Look-a there. Whoo, my hands are cold."

Uncle Jack snapped off the feet, chopped off the head with his hatchet, sliced the belly open with his pocketknife, and pulled out the guts, which Henry knew he'd smell in a second or two. The guts rolled in Uncle Jack's hand like tiny sausage bags of jelly and steamed in the cold air.

"Look at that little heart," said Uncle Jack.

They skinned the other rabbit, then pulled up water from the well, poured some into a pan, washed both rabbits, and dried them with a white rag.

1941

———

Carson stayed with Henry for a few days after the family reunion, before Uncle Samuel took him and Aunt Linda back to Florida. On their first night in bed together, as soon as the house was quiet, Carson asked, "Do you ever jack off?"

"Is that the same thing as beating your meat?" asked Henry.

"Yeah."

"I think I've done it, but Uncle Jack says that when you get older something comes out called 'sum,' and it's got some kind of fertilizer in it that goes in a woman and then she lays a egg in some place inside of her body where the baby comes out of into this sack that she keeps in her stomach for ninety days."

"Sum?"

"Something like that. And the real name is serum or something."

"Did you ever see him and Aunt Dorie doing it?"

"What?"

"Making sex," said Carson.

"Yeah — one time. I thought they were fighting. There was this grunting."

"Who called it beating your meat?" asked Carson.

"Uncle Jack. He told me his mama told him he'd go blind if he did it, and so he asked her could he do it till he started wearing glasses."

"What does that mean?"

"I don't know."

"Does he wear glasses?"

"No. Do you know what a goiter is?" asked Henry.

"No."

"It's something that makes a big ball in your neck like that man Yancy down the road has. The one I showed you at the store. Remember?"

"Oh yeah."

"Do you think God would care if you beat your meat in a dream?"

"If you *dreamed* you did? Or if you did it *while* you were dreaming?" asked Carson.

"If you dreamed you did it."

"I don't know. It wouldn't be your fault. I guess that would be God's fault."

"But Aunt Dorie said don't do it. The Bible says don't do it somewhere in there."

"That's what Daddy said too," said Carson.

"I bet he didn't call it beating your meat."

"Naw. He called it playing with yourself."

"You think God forgave you?" asked Henry.

"Yeah, since I asked him. That's all you have to do."

"You have to mean it."

"Oh yeah, I know that."

Henry sat in a chair near Yancy's bed. Yancy lay with his eyes closed and the death rattle in his chest, a sound with both ice and warmth in it, a rattle that if Yancy could wake up, maybe he could just sit up and cough out, Henry figured. Mrs. Albright was talking about Pearl Harbor, and Henry couldn't quite understand. Somebody had bombed a pearl.

Yancy was lying on his back in his bed, covered up, and his face looked smaller and whiter, and his nose longer than usual. Mrs. Albright had had his bed moved into the living room, close to the kitchen, so that she wouldn't have to go back and forth so far, and Henry wondered about Yancy not liking the cats. But now he seemed like he was asleep, but maybe he would wake up, since his chest and throat were making that noise.

Aunt Dorie sat down beside Henry. Mrs. Albright walked over and sat in a chair nearby. There were some neighbors in the room that Henry didn't know very well. Uncle Jack was eating a biscuit and a chicken leg. He sat at the kitchen table. He'd come down to help move the bed the day before.

Mrs. Albright said, "Henry, son, Yancy might not make it. And if he don't, he'll go on up to heaven, and that's where we'll all be, where we can all meet, where I'll see him again and be able to take care of him."

Thomas the cat smelled Death up in the ceiling near the stovepipe. He looked. It was big and yellow and like a cave, darker in the middle.

Henry thought about Yancy not having a daddy either, about his own daddy being in heaven, about Saint Peter at the gates of heaven. Before Henry could stop his mouth, he said, "Will he have the goiter?"

"The goiter? Well, yes, if he wants to, if God wants him to, and I bet God will leave it up to Yancy," said Mrs. Albright. "Well, no. I bet he won't have it. Because Yancy never did like that thing while he was down here on earth. So he won't have it in heaven. God will damn it. It will be a God-damned goiter." She looked around. Nobody minded. Nobody was looking at her. She said, a little louder, "It will be a God-damned goiter, because it will go to hell."

"Praise the Lord," said Uncle Jack from the kitchen, food in his mouth.

A couple of people looked in on Mrs. Albright from the kitchen.

In a single bound up from the floor, Paul landed on the foot of the bed. Mrs. Albright stood, stepped over, scatted him back down. "Git away, Paul," she said.

Paul strode over to the far side of the wood box and sat. Both his ears twitched, one then the other. He settled down — squatted on his back legs, then kind of collapsed onto his front ones like a dog. "It's so sad his daddy didn't live longer," he said.

"My daddy was always so serious," said Isaac, "kind of looking off at things."

"*That* he did," said Judas.

"Hush, you bad man," said Paul.

"Sometimes I think I couldn't help it," said Judas.

"Be happy," said Angel. "Rejoice. Yancy's in heaven."

Jack stepped in. "Them cats talking again, Mrs. Albright?"

"Oh yes, they get to mumbling now and then. I always wished Yancy had liked them more."

"Let's head on up the road, buddy," Jack said to Henry. "Well, there's some people just don't take to cats, Mrs. Albright," he said, as Mrs. Albright stood.

"I don't think you and Yancy felt much different on that, Jack," she said.

"Well, no ma'am. I don't guess we did. I like a animal that'll come when you call it. You let us know, now, if we can do anything."

As they walked up the road, Jack said, "I'm glad your Aunt Dorie has taught you to be good to old people, buddy. Way down the line, if you're lucky, it'll come back around."

"She said it was wrong to steal, even from rich people."

"Oh, she did. Well, she's probably right. I just need to even things up sometimes."

✵   ✵   ✵

When Aunt Dorie took him down front at the church to see Yancy dead, Mrs. Albright was sitting in a chair at the head of the coffin, and she was crying. Flowers were on stands, and in the air was that sweet, perfumelike funeral flower smell. The coffin was a shiny wood one, one of the ones made by Mr. Fitzhugh at the furniture store, and Yancy wore a light gray coat and a white shirt with a red tie. Old Mrs. House, with her black cane, walked up, looked at Yancy a minute, then said to Mrs. Albright, "I like that red tie. It gives him a little color in his complexion." She turned back and looked at Yancy. "They do get pale at a time like this."

Henry looked in at pale Yancy. He wondered if the ball was going to be a different color than it had been. But there was no sign of the ball.

Mrs. Albright reached over, pulled Henry to her. She smelled the same way still. "Oh Henry," she said, "he loved you so much, and you should get his train. That's just what he would have wanted."

"Where's his ball?" Henry asked.

"Henry," said Aunt Dorie.

"That's okay, Dorie." She turned to Henry. "Dr. Block told me that he'd cut it out if Yancy died, so he did."

Yancy's sister was at the funeral too, but she didn't sit down beside the coffin with Mrs. Albright. She came in with the family, though, when they came in to sit in the first few pews at the beginning of the service. Her head was held up so high it was like it was leaning back. Uncle Jack had been talking about her again, said she was mad because she never got the attention Yancy got. He said if she'd been able to work herself up a goiter she would have fit in better.

The scripture for the sermon was Isaiah 25:8 — "He will swallow up death in victory." Preacher Gibson preached that it was not a time for sadness, but for happiness, that Yancy was in heaven, rejoicing with the saints, and that it was never too late for anybody in the congregation to surrender to Jesus so as to join Yancy in the company of God and Jesus for eternity, and that only through Jesus Christ could anybody ever get to heaven.

At Mrs. Albright's house after the funeral, all the cats were home, but not too many people were around. Plates of food rested on the kitchen table. Aunt Dorie fixed Henry a plate with two chicken wings, some black-eyed peas, turnip greens, and some thin fried corn bread. She gave him the dish of banana pudding before he finished eating his main food, and he didn't remember that ever happening before.

After he ate, Henry walked into Yancy's room and looked at the closed closet door, the yellow curtains, the chest of drawers with a few hats and a trophy of some kind on top, and the floor lamp and straight-back chair.

Mrs. Albright led Aunt Dorie into the room. Aunt Dorie looked a little worried about something. Mrs. Albright said, "I just had to . . ." and she pointed to Yancy's Red Rider wagon. His electric train was in it. "I need to set this back up. I can't let it go yet. I know Yancy would want you to have it, Henry, but I need to set it back up. And I found out I can't bring myself to get rid of any of his clothes for a while either. I just — it feels like, like he's still in here."

"I can understand that," said Aunt Dorie. "I can understand that." She looked around.

"It was his body, Dorie," said Mrs. Albright. "His body was so tender and white, and his skin was so soft. He was like an angel. Didn't you think so?" She was rubbing her arm.

"I sure do. Yancy was a good boy . . . man."

"I just forgot about his skin. You know, his body. I hadn't looked at it in such a long time. I hadn't touched it and felt it and all that. His face was always kind of red, you know, but his skin underneath his clothes was different. He'd got so he took care of hisself and gave hisself a bath." She looked around the room. "I ain't been able to stop thinking about his body since we dressed him out."

Henry remembered that Jesus had raised one of his friends, Lazarus, from the dead, and a little girl too. Those were lucky people. That would be magic, though, wouldn't it? But Jesus could do magic. "Are any of the cats named Lazarus?" he asked Mrs. Albright.

"No, son. I don't have a Lazarus. But that's a good idea, when another'n comes round. Or maybe I can rename Judas. He's so unlucky. You know, he learned his lesson too late, way too late. But sometimes I think: Where would we be without him?"

1942

Henry knew that it was going to happen, that Jesus would call him down to the front of the church after a service to accept him. Nobody could be exactly sure when it would happen. And if Jesus didn't call him, then he'd just wait some more. But most everybody in his family was pretty young when they were called, except Uncle Jack had come from Strickland County, and his family didn't know Jesus for some reason that had to do with being common.

So on the first Sunday morning in April, when the dogwoods — with the flower that was the cross — and the wisteria were just coming into bloom, and Aunt Dorie was all the time talking about the runted dogwood, because that was the wood of Jesus' cross — after the regular service, and during the invitational hymn, Henry, after Aunt Dorie had talked to him one more time, and after he had thanked God for Jesus the night before while he prayed for a long time on his knees by the bed with his knee against the bed pot while Uncle Jack was out at the canning shed smoking a cigar, and after Caroline talked to Henry about her giving *her* life to Jesus — after all this, on that next Sunday morning, Henry stepped out into the aisle and in spite of Uncle Jack's talk about no magic and all that in Trixie's Bible, in spite of having played with his woody and been chastised by Aunt Dorie while being given the go-ahead by Uncle Jack in some way or another, in spite of being caught stealing a stick of licorice from Mr. Jackson's store, in spite of getting caught saying "damn" at school twice, Henry, on that Sunday morning, experienced Jesus walking before him, leading the way in a white robe, on the rug that was red — the color of Jesus' blood — and he followed Jesus on down to the outstretched arms of Preacher Gibson, who welcomed him into the community of Christians, into the community of people in the world who would be spared the fires of hell and instead be swept up into heaven, where there would be no mean people, to live in the presence of God and Jesus and all the saints, walking streets of gold for eternity.

The next day in school Henry drew a sketch of Jesus crying, big tears coming down his face. When Aunt Dorie saw it and asked him why Jesus was crying, he said because of all the sin in the world, and that Jesus had been singing "The

Old Rugged Cross," probably. Aunt Dorie said she wanted that song sung at her funeral.

Then he drew pictures of crosses on hills, and then on flat land, and just after he'd drawn a cross in class Mrs. Peebles showed him how he could draw a line from left to right about halfway up the cross, behind it, and there was a whole different and grown-up look to it. It was a horizon line, she said.

Mrs. Peebles was the one who said in class that she didn't know why preachers had to shout, and Henry couldn't understand why they wouldn't shout. He wondered if she might be going to hell.

Then one day Mrs. Peebles showed Henry how to draw a box, and he asked her if she'd show him how to draw Jesus on a cross, and she said she'd like to show him how to draw an airplane and a car, and so he started drawing *them* a lot. Later she showed him how to draw a ship so that it looked like it was on real water.

The electricity had been out for two days on account of a bad summer storm. Henry smelled the kerosene lantern in his sleep, it seemed like, and was then awake, seeing Uncle Jack pull up a chair beside his bed, sit down, set the lantern on the floor. It cast shadows upward. Where was Aunt Dorie? Henry sensed a lateness in the night — or maybe it was early, still dark, morning.

"I need to tell you something, shortstop." Uncle Jack wore a shirt with flaps on the pockets. In the lantern light,

Henry couldn't tell if the shirt was blue or brown. Besides alcohol, Uncle Jack smelled like cigars and the inside of the truck. Henry watched, wondering, as Uncle Jack coughed gently with his hand over his mouth, then said, "Old Uncle Jack is going to have to move on down the road. I'm going to have to look for work down in Pinehurst, maybe. I done got my bus ticket. I'm leaving the truck, and as soon as you're a little older you can drive it. Caroline can drive it all she wants right now."

"But why —"

"No, no, stop, I ain't going to be able to answer no questions, because I've kinda got in over my head, and if I stick around it'll be sure enough trouble coming, and it's all my fault. Don't you start in now. You're too big for that. Everything's going to be all right. Hush up, son, don't be doing that. Hush, now. I got to go. I'll be back in touch soon. Uncle Jack's going to stay in touch."

He bent over, kissed Henry on the forehead. He'd never done that before. He'd taken the matchstick out of his mouth. He stood and blew out the lantern, and left, not looking back as he closed the door quietly. Henry could see candles lit in the kitchen. After the door closed, white spots remained in his vision, then faded.

The next day, Saturday, Aunt Dorie kept Henry inside all day. She recited the Twenty-third Psalm several times, then the Lord's Prayer, and asked Henry to join her in more praying. Sometimes they both prayed in silence and sometimes she prayed aloud that God would be with her and Henry. Henry followed her from room to room as she cleaned and cleaned, again and again. At one point she said, "Come in here and sit down with me on the couch." He sat beside her, and she looked straight ahead out the window by the fireplace for a minute and then turned to him and said, "I want you to know what our vows said. They said 'for better, for worse; for richer, for poorer; in sickness and in health; to love and to cherish, till death us do part.' That's what they said."

"What are vows?"

"They are things that are stronger than a promise."

"Is that like a covenant?"

"Yes, it is."

1944

———

A few months after Pa D's funeral, Uncle Samuel moved from his orange groves in Florida to the homeplace — to raise tobacco — and brought Carson, fifteen, his youngest, the only child left at home. Aunt Linda had died two years earlier after getting and losing cancer several times.

Soon after Linda got sick the first time, years earlier, Samuel began to think of Dorie in sensual ways, and prayed for forgiveness. At the family reunions each year he flirted with her, and she did not dissuade him. She'd always wished Jack were as devout as Samuel. Samuel was so steady and predictable, and though he didn't smile much, he always had a smile for her. She could afford to like him in a slightly flirtatious way, because he visited the homeplace only a few days each year and was then gone. She felt so sorry for Linda, who had never seemed fully well. And there in the last year she felt sorry for Samuel having to watch Linda get weaker and weaker.

Each year, back in Florida after the family reunion, Samuel seemed to think about Dorie a little longer than he had the year before. Once Linda died and he'd come back to Simmons and moved into the homeplace with Carson, the courtship was direct and simple. He visited her twice, then asked her to marry him, and she said yes.

She needed a man, and in her view he was exactly the moral guide that Henry needed — had needed all along.

Disadvantages for Henry — the lectures, scolding, sermons — were balanced by the fact that he and Carson lived under the same roof.

Uncle Samuel increased the tobacco acreage to include most of the farm and paid Caroline and Henry thirty-five cents an hour to help out during that first summer after he married Aunt Dorie.

Ma D, getting more feeble by the month, moved in with Caroline and Aunt Ruth when Pa D died. Caroline began working at the Simmons drugstore, in addition to the tobacco fields, saving money for Woman's College in Greensboro. She wanted to be a schoolteacher.

Jimmy Tilletson — a distant cousin just moved back from Tennessee and now a hired hand on the homeplace — had bad teeth and a GI haircut that he said he would keep as long as his brothers were overseas. He and his wife, Jeanette, had a little girl who had polio. Aunt Dorie said the little girl's dresses were dirty. They brought her to church, and the men who were ushers each Sunday lifted her in her wheelchair up the steps. Jeanette worked at the cotton mill, and Mrs. Albright kept the daughter on workdays. Although two of Jimmy's brothers were soldiers in the war, the army had not taken Jimmy. No one seemed to know why. Jimmy said it was because he was flat-footed, but when he climbed barefoot into the tobacco barn rafters to hang tobacco, anybody could see he had arches.

While they were frog gigging one night, just the three of them, Jimmy told Henry and Carson about handling snakes in his church in Tennessee. Mark 16:18 promised that believers wouldn't get bit when they picked up snakes. Jimmy had seen plenty of snakes held up over believers' heads while they shouted to God in the unknown tongues that Mark 16:17 talked about. He said his church had to keep it all secret because of the newspaper.

"Why couldn't he tell about it?" Henry asked after he and Carson were in bed. They had twin beds in their own bedroom now. "I didn't understand that part."

"Because all the churches have these things they don't want other churches to know about. Like the Catholics sprinkle people instead of baptize. There's a Catholic church up in Raleigh and a Jewish church. And I think there's some Jewish churches in McNeill too."

"Are they the same as the Jews in the Bible?"

"I don't know. These might be new Jews. I think they are."

"Do *they* sprinkle?"

"I don't know."

"Why do they want to keep it a secret?"

"Because it's connected to some kind of code that only preachers can know. Like the Morse code. Like in the army they have these codes that the Germans and Japs don't have. The Jews had a code and then the Christians had a code. I think."

"If we went in the army and got killed, would that make Aunt Dorie a gold star mother?"

"No, because you have to be the real mother."

Henry thought about his real mother somewhere in Raleigh, a blue flag with a gold star hanging in her window. He pictured the flag in a window of a building he'd once passed in Raleigh on a school trip. It was a nice house that had TOURISTS written on a sign out front, and he thought she might live there. He thought about the letter and present he got from Uncle Jack. "I got something in the mail today. You want to see?"

"Sure. What is it?"

Henry opened his drawer, got out his billfold, and pulled three gold packs from the hidden cash pocket. "Three preventatives. Well, I got this billfold too. It's all from Uncle Jack. He wrote me a letter, told me how to hide them in the secret cash place and move them around so they wouldn't make circles in the leather, and he told me I needed to learn to use them so I could avoid misery."

"They keep you from getting a girl pregnant," said Carson.

"I know it."

"And they're rubbers, not preventatives. You ever seen a water bomb made out of one?"

"Yeah, I guess I did. I don't know. You want these?"

"You don't want them?" asked Carson.

"No."

"Why?"

"I'm not going to do it before I get married."

"Why not?"

"I promised Aunt Dorie. You're not supposed to. The Bible says not to — somewhere in there. But Uncle Jack said you could practice on a banana."

"Screw a *banana?*"

"No, dummy. Put a *rubber* on one."

"I'll be right back," said Carson. He came back with a banana.

"Should we peel it?" asked Henry.

"Peel it? I don't think so. Do you know how to unhook a bra strap?"

"No. Why?"

"It ain't easy. You need to practice."

"But I won't be doing it."

"Doing what?"

"Sex. All the way."

"Aw, come on. Then you can play with their titties. Ain't you ever read Song of Solomon, this king in the Bible? David's daddy?"

"No."

"Everybody knew about that in Florida. Hand me your Bible."

Henry got his Bible off his dresser.

Carson read and Henry listened.

"That's really there? Let me see it." Henry looked over the passage.

"Okay," said Carson. "I'm going to get a bra out of the dirty clothes basket."

"It's Aunt Dorie's."

"I know that . . . aw, come on."

Carson left and returned. "Here it is." He held it from one end so that it hung lengthwise toward the floor. "You want to go first?"

"Go first?"

"Try to unhook it. You're supposed to practice with it *on* somebody."

"I don't need to practice."

"Aw, come on."

Henry looked at the door. Then the window. "Okay. You can practice."

"Take off your pajama top."

"Why?"

"Because you wouldn't wear a bra over a shirt, stupid."

"Something ain't right about this." Henry took off his pajama top.

"Here. Put your arms through. Okay. Good." Carson studied the clasp, then fit the ends together so they held.

Henry raised his arms and turned in a circle. "What do you think?" He looked in the dresser mirror as he turned.

"Pretty good," said Carson. "They stuff them with toilet paper to make falsies."

"How do you know that?"

"I just do."

"Why wouldn't they use handkerchiefs?"

"Maybe some of them do. Now you got to face me."

"Why?"

"Because I'm not going to be standing *behind* her, stupid. You think I'm going to *sneak up* on her or something?"

Two taps on the door. Aunt Dorie's voice: "What you-all doing in there?"

"Nothing," said Carson.

She opened the door.

PART V

_____

REVELATION

1950

———

An hour south of Tallahassee and a few miles north of Panakala lay the twenty-two-thousand-acre Palmetto Greens Plantation. The main house stood at the end of a long, wide driveway. Tall oaks grew out over the drive. Lawns were green year-round. The dirt-and-rock driveway, dragged periodically with a weighted pallet behind a tractor — years ago dragged with a weighted pallet behind a mule — was not the washed-out tan color of other sand in the area. It was, rather, the rich brown of a deer rump, kept that way by a clay mixture, added from time to time.

Along the driveway, beyond the oaks, sat small barns, horse stalls, dog pens for the English pointers, and houses for the tenants and the overseer, all painted every fourth year. On the property were tennis courts, a golf course, and a train stop. A rail loop from the Seaboard Air Line Railway had been arranged. Several times a month during quail season, hunters arrived from New York or Washington.

The plantation raised cotton and corn with tenant help, but its main purpose was to entertain quail hunters, mostly from New York and Washington, DC. It was owned by O. L. "Ossie" Greenlove, a prominent New York businessman and criminal. Greenlove had hired Teddy Lamont, one of Blinky's lieutenants, to head his security force, not knowing Teddy remained on Blinky's payroll. In Greenlove's office, a five-foot-tall safe held antique handguns, gold coins, Confederate paper money, historical documents, and swords, all of which Mr. Greenlove enjoyed showing to guests. The safe also held acquisitions he never showed: cash, and rare documents that were to be sold on the black market.

On a Sunday morning in late June, before daylight, Clearwater and Henry walked slowly beneath the plantation house — it was that high off the ground — Clearwater shining light from a flashlight onto the joists and underflooring along the approximate reverse route of the safe, especially on the porch, in order to determine if the floor would support the weight of a forklift and large safe, even though if all went well they wouldn't need the forklift. Were the joists sufficiently close together and sturdy?

Only certain kinds of angle problems might require use of the forklift — for example, if the incline from porch to truck bed was too steep for managing the safe by hand. Teddy Lamont's written assessment suggested the loading job could be done by hand, using a hydraulic jack and minimal tools and equipment, but Blinky long ago learned to require a forklift and dump truck on-site for any safe job. He'd had them on hand, after all, since his and Clearwater's creative thievery during the war. You never could tell when you might need them. Besides, they were a tax write-off.

Underneath the house, directly below the safe, several two-by-six boards were already secured between and across joists.

"Now why the hell is all that there?" asked Clearwater.

"For support?" said Henry.

"I suppose . . . I hope. Because if he's" — he moved around, shined the flashlight at different angles — "if he's got the safe bolted down, then we might have problems. But Lamont didn't say nothing about that in the folder."

A few minutes later, Clearwater, carrying hammer, nails, and two of four sheets of plywood, entered through the front door. Lamont had supplied a key. A Ford Motor Company trademark was printed on each sheet of plywood, along with FORKLIFT COUNTERWEIGHT.

Henry stood in the truck bed, shined his light across two axes, a service station hydraulic car jack, two heavy forklift pallets, leather straps and ropes, plywood, iron-pipe axles, five small metal wheels, a large khaki-green canvas tarp, a block and tackle, three long lengths of logging chain, lengths of smaller chain, chain cutter, toolbox, metal lay-down tracks, sixteen-pound sledge hammer, two hatchets, other tools and equipment, and a pouch of twenty-dollar bills. Pushing the hydraulic jack in front of him, Henry started along one of the wide, iron-pipe-reinforced gangplanks from the truck to the porch.

Around back, near the open back door, sat the Chrysler. Clearwater had both sets of its keys. There were two directions for a getaway. One, out the driveway to the main highway — to use if they finished as planned, before daylight — and the back way, in case they left after daybreak or due to some other unexpected problem. The back way would take them along a wagon path and onto a two-lane blacktop.

Just inside the front door, Henry met Clearwater coming out. "The goddamned safe is bolted to the floor. We're going to have to . . . I don't know." He looked at Henry. "This is *not* my doing."

After some hacking and hammering under the house, Clearwater exposed a couple of bolts and nuts. "Oh God, the nuts are welded to the bolts." It crossed his mind that he was being set up. He walked out from under the house, stood, listened carefully for a full thirty seconds. No, it was that stupid Teddy Lamont. *He never even checked to see if the safe was bolted to the floor. The idiot.*

Clearwater walked back. "We're going to have to . . ."

"We could probably do something with the block and tackle," said Henry.

"Like what?"

"Well, I don't know without thinking about it."

"Block and tackle are not going to help us. We're going to have to chop around the damn thing, free it, and let it fall into the truck." He looked at Henry. "We can back under there far enough, I think. You got any better ideas?"

"We could use the logging chain and pull it out — like pulling a tooth. Out through the window somehow."

"I don't think we got enough logging chain." How the hell did he get himself in a position to be listening to a *boy* for ideas? "Go get the truck. We'll back it under here. Wait. We got to get the forklift out of the truck bed. Drive it off onto the porch. Can you do that?"

"Sure, but what if we just drive the forklift up against the back of the cab — take off the tines? That would save time, and that still leaves room."

"Okay. Do that. Hurry up."

Now Henry had the truck in reverse and was looking through the big driver's-side rearview mirror. Clearwater directed with his arms. Henry backed over a flower bed, up to the latticework.

"Back on through it!" shouted Clearwater. He stepped under the house, said to himself, "We're lucky them pillars are placed right."

Henry heard the lattice wood popping.

"Come on," said Clearwater. "Come on. Okay. Stop!"

When Henry stepped on the brakes he could see Clearwater in the sideview mirror, bathed in red light, standing under the house. He climbed down from the truck, walked under. Clearwater opened the truck tailgate, got out an ax. The safe was above the rear of the truck bed.

Up in Greenlove's office, after they'd axed through the floor on the two sides of the safe that ran parallel to the joists, they started on the third side.

"It's almost daylight," said Clearwater. "We got to get on the damn road."

Henry thought about how normal citizens had no idea what-all the FBI did. This was risky. Real criminals would get very upset at being robbed. He and Clearwater couldn't afford mistakes. "What if the safe drops and then goes right on through the floor of the truck bed?"

Clearwater stood, his hand on the ax handle, sweat dripping from his nose. "I don't think . . . There were some fence posts piled out there. God almighty. Line the bed."

At about daylight, the safe started through the floor with a loud cracking sound, broke loose, and fell on its side onto the fence posts lying in the truck bed, bounced once. They covered it with canvas and tied it with rope. On the canvas, stamped in large letters, was FORKLIFT COUNTERWEIGHT.

Safely away, driving the Chrysler, following the dump truck northeast along the old Atlanta highway, Clearwater began considering his options.

In a couple of hours, he and Henry sat across from each other at a small table with a red-checkered tablecloth. Clearwater was eating a waffle. Henry, pancakes, a scrambled egg, and grits.

"One of the things I was thinking about when we drove away," said Henry, "is why didn't we have about thirty FBI agents helping us out, just in case? You know, just go ahead and act like a army instead of a couple of guys. Then I figured maybe . . . I don't know, why not?"

"This whole operation — the big plan — has to stay so hush-hush a lot of the FBI people don't even know what's going on. And when these guys get arrested, people will never know the FBI was even involved."

"But idn't this a *different* gang?"

"Listen. They're interrelated in ways I don't know about yet. In ways Blinky don't even know about. This is just like the army. You follow orders." Clearwater sopped a piece of waffle in syrup. "You don't ask questions. Somebody up above knows more than you. If they don't, then you're in the wrong army. And we're in the right army. So we just do our job."

"Is there any chance we could stop in Jeffries for lunch," said Henry, "or just stop and pick up some fruit?"

"Your fruit stand? Your woman?"

"Yes sir. Right close to the Night's Rest Motel — just down the road from it — where we stayed. Maybe we could stay there tonight."

"We're staying in Brownlee. At the cabin camp."

"Then maybe we could just stop for an apple or something."

"We'll see how we do on time."

"A grape."

Clearwater was a little worried about returning to Brownlee — that truck stop and bar. He visualized the man turning away, his feet planted, the movement of his leg as he lay on the ground. But now the car jack was buried, and nobody had seen him. Nobody alive. And nobody could trace a car jack anyway. He remembered the waitress, red-and-gray hair. That's what got him thinking about getting him some romance. He thought about Caroline's neck, about her willingness, her weakness, her begging him to promise to never tell Henry.

He thought about Blinky. One time Blinky said that thinking small was one of Clearwater's problems. Blinky had always been a little too cocky.

Marleen watched as a dump truck pulled in and stopped. It was late Sunday afternoon. Henry had called Friday night and said there was a fifty-fifty chance he might stop by — could she be at the fruit stand even though it was Sunday? She said of course. A car pulled in and stopped beside the dump truck. And . . . it was *Henry* stepping down from the truck.

She walked out to meet him. They hugged and kissed.

Clearwater stood in front of the Chrysler and called to Henry.

"I'll be right back," Henry said to Marleen.

"Okay, here's the plan," said Clearwater. "Here are the car keys. You know from the maps how to get to the cabin camp. I'll take the dump truck. You need to come in the morning. Not before. Stay wherever you want to." He looked at Marleen, smiled a little. He reached for his billfold. "Here's a hundred and fifty on the gig, and you'll get another one-fifty tomorrow. Show up at seven-thirty in the morning. Don't be late. I'll be sitting on my porch steps. If you don't see me, just wait."

"Okay," said Henry. "Don't you want to meet my girl-friend, Marleen?"

"No. I don't want to meet Marleen. Get your stuff out of the truck. Seven-thirty sharp, now."

"Yes sir."

Just after dark that night, when Henry got to the wagon path behind the fruit stand, he stopped, felt in his pockets to see if he'd forgotten anything. He had preventatives, his flashlight, his small flask of whiskey, and the army blanket from the closet shelf at the motel. This was it. His legs felt weak. Besides all else, she was bringing him a poem.

He met her on the path, saw her before she saw him, and stepped behind a tree that stood right up against the path. When she got there, he said in a hard whisper, "Marleen."

She gave a little startled cry and stepped away from him. She had on a long skirt and a blouse with the shirttail out — he couldn't tell the color in the moonlight — and a purse on a long strap over her shoulder. He stepped into the path.

"I brought us a blanket," he said. "It's a nice night out."

"I would have dressed up more, but my mama might have thought something. I'll be glad when you can meet her — and the rest."

"Me too. Hold my hand."

*   *   *

Clearwater and Blinky sat on Clearwater's screened-in porch at the cabin camp. It was dark, about ten minutes until nine. Blinky had time to look over the safe and talk over the next gig: the doctor down in Drain. The next morning he'd drive the truck and safe up to McNeill to get it opened.

A pair of binoculars lay in Blinky's lap. When Blinky arrived, Clearwater had told him about the woman over in cabin twelve. On the hour she would open her blind and stand there naked.

They waited on the porch in the dark. Blinky lit a cigar, and they talked about the old times and the weather.

"Okay," said Clearwater. He looked at his watch.

Blinky leaned forward, elbows on knees, pressing the binoculars to his eyes.

Clearwater stood. "It's about time," he said. "Like I said, it'll go pretty fast. I'll be right back. Just watch, you ain't going to believe it."

On his bed was his crowbar.

They walked along the wagon path together until she took him by the hand, glory hallelujah, and led him off the path to a grassy area about the size of a room, on a knoll, with some big rocks around. He spread the blanket and they sat facing each other. She pulled a bottle of mosquito oil and a paperback book from her purse. "I got some mosquito oil here, and I can't wait to read you this poem," she said.

"Me either."

"Okay." She opened the book and pulled out a piece of paper. "Do you want me to read it? Or do you want to read it with your flashlight?"

"Here." He handed her the flashlight. "You read it."

"Here goes," she said.

If I was the bark upon a tree and you were the wood
 within, every morning when I woke up, you'd be
 under my skin.
Or you're a tree and I'm the grass below, and comes
 lightning and thunder too; then in the middle of
 the storm, I'll be safe under you.
Or if I'm a pea in the soup and you're the butter bean,
 then we'll always be together, even after the pot
 is clean.
Or if I'm the bottom of the ocean, and you're the deep
 blue sea, every morning when I wake up, there
 you'll be, on me.
So when we're apart, I'm a bee without a buzz,
If we take different paths, I'm a peach without the fuzz.

"Gosh," said Henry. "That's just like if it was out of a book."

"It's a love poem."

Henry felt his breath almost leave.

"I started it with just the part about the peach fuzz because, you remember, we talked about that, and it kind of wrote itself backwards, and it was like somebody else was writing it, and so, here, it's a gift." She handed him the piece of paper.

"I . . . thank you."

"I didn't know if I'd ever see you again."

"I knew I'd see you again." Henry thought about all those grapes and fronds and things in Song of Solomon, the two Israelites visiting the prostitute. He was okay. Maybe he should . . . He handed her the flask. Without speaking, she took a short drink.

"I'm going to need some of that mosquito oil," he said.

She reached for the bottle, twisted off the cap.

"What is it?" he asked.

"Alcohol and castor oil. It's what Grandma always mixed. Are all your grandparents alive?"

"Just two," said Henry. "Well, one now, that I know about. Maybe three. The other two that I'm not sure about used to live in South Carolina, but I never met them."

She lightly dabbed oil on her neck, arms, ankles, then leaned over and said, "Here, let's get you. I'll do it." She dabbed his arms and neck, leaned close while she was doing that, and so he found courage to place his hand on her cheek like he'd seen Audie Murphy do, and kiss her on the mouth. Her lips opened readily and she leaned back, pulling him with her. She put her lips to his ear. "Will you be my teddy bear?" she whispered, and laughed her big laugh.

She lay on her back on the army blanket, and he lay on his stomach beside her, his head over hers, kissing her. After a while of that, she pulled her head away from the kiss and put her lips to his ear and with one hand rubbed the back of his neck lightly. She nibbled his earlobe. He turned onto his side, got his hand up under her blouse, moved his hand around behind and found the clasp. She was staying happy. He pinched it like Carson had said. It remained attached. She reached behind and touched it and it sprang loose, and she guided his hand around to the front and onto a big breast and a nipple that was standing up, hard as a marble. And as big, it felt like. He was in the middle of some kind of carnival, some kind of state fair with all the horns blowing and balloons popping and crowds shouting. She was unbuttoning with an urgency.

He placed his mouth on her neck. She gently pushed his head on down toward her breast.

"Bite it," she said.

"Bite it?"

"It's okay. I bite it myself."

"Your neck's that long?"

"No. My titty's kind of big." She laughed her laugh, big and easy, like a waterfall.

"I've got a preventative," he said.

"I broke the goddamned binoculars," said Clearwater — to himself. Blinky lay on the floor, not moving. He'd had to hit him more than a couple of times, and he didn't like that. But he could take the rug away. He'd had to move it out there from inside.

*   *   *

"I'm sorry it was so fast," said Henry. He was looking up into the boughs of a long-leaf pine. He'd just felt the moon speeding up, faster and faster around the earth, until its orbit melted into liquid silver. The heated orbit then collapsed into itself and fell long and slow into an ocean somewhere, and cooled.

"That's okay." She was a little out of breath.

She unstraddled, leaned toward him, their lips met, then she sat back up straight.

"I think I can do it again," he said.

"Oh, I hope so." She started adjusting her clothes. "Have you ever seen a television?"

"I saw one in Atlanta at Sears and Roebuck. Why?"

"Just something to talk about for a minute. I've seen plenty of pictures of them. In magazines. At my sister's."

"I love you."

"Oh, Henry, I love you too. So much. What are we going to do?"

"What do you mean?"

"I don't know," said Marleen.

"You want to come on up to the motel?"

"Why not?" She laughed. "Henry, you don't like me less because of this, do you?"

"Less? Lord, no. And listen. I don't know why I told you that about my heart. My heart's fine. Do you like me less because I made that up?"

"No. I was planning to ask you about that. You look too healthy to have heart problems."

"I met this Bible salesman that claimed he had heart problems, but he looked like he did."

"Are you sure you have to leave in the morning?"

"I've got to be at the cabin camp on the Okaloga at seven-thirty, but after next weekend, I'm going to have some time off, I think, and I'm going to buy a 'thirty-nine Ford roadster, and you can look for me to come driving up."

"I want you to meet my sister," she said.

"I want you to meet my sister."

"How far is it from here up to Simmons?" asked Marleen.

"Not that far. A few hours. Maybe nine."

"Oh, Henry." She moved into his arms, her head against his shoulder.

At seven-fifteen Monday morning, Henry passed Mrs. Finley and Miss Sarah's house, just up from the cabin camp. Mrs. Finley was on the porch. He would stop for a few minutes and not be late to meet Clearwater.

Henry stood in the yard and talked to her about the squash she was getting from their garden. Then Mrs. Finley said, "Come on in a minute and see Sarah."

"I need to get on. I just got a minute."

"I can feed you a good sausage biscuit."

Henry opened the screen door for her, and inside, Sarah sat in the living room. She said, "Well, look what the cat drug up."

"I was just passing by. I ain't got but a minute. But I can't pass up a sausage and biscuit."

"Go on in there and get it."

While he ate, Mrs. Finley and Miss Sarah escorted him back out onto the porch. "We were worried about you," said Mrs. Finley, "because a man got shot up at the truck stop that night we got back from Jeffries. We even called the sheriff to be sure it won't you. It was some poor truck driver from up north. Somebody stole a car jack then shot him. That's all they could figure out."

"That's too bad. I got to run. But I'll be back before too long when I come through on the way down to see Marleen."

"That'll be just fine," said Mrs. Finley. "You bring her on by here and we'll feed her something."

"Keep your nose clean," said Miss Sarah.

Henry put the gear lever in reverse, raised his arm onto the back of the front seat. He was thinking about that truck driver. There was something that he couldn't quite put together.

Clearwater sat on the steps at the cabin camp.

The dump truck and the canvas-wrapped safe were securely stored in a warehouse in Brownlee. The warehouse owner, given his remuneration, would be happy to hold on to it for a few days.

The depth of the Okaloga River, in a sharp bend a mile downstream from the cabin camp, was over twenty feet. On the bottom lay ancient potsherds that looked like small rocks to the nonexpert. Rock-sharpening tools from thousands of years earlier were bathed in green scum, the tendrils of which moved in the river current as if alive. Nearby, in the dark gray underwater morning light, lay two forklift pallets, a set of forklift tines, and a sixteen-pound sledge hammer, all secured with heavy logging chain to the ankle of a short naked man.

The riverbank above appeared undisturbed.

Henry pulled up at seven thirty-five.

"You're late," said Clearwater.

"I know it. I'm sorry. My breakfast went just a little bit long."

"Let's go."

"The truck is gone already?" asked Henry.

"Blinky took it back."

"Did you get my cast net out of the floorboard?"

"It's right here on the porch with my stuff."

On the road to Drain, Henry wondered if Clearwater would ask him about Marleen, about the night before. He wasn't sure what he might say. He couldn't bring it up himself, but he'd have to say something if asked.

"We've got to do some careful planning," said Clearwater. "This guy is a big operator like the one we just did, and it'll be another three hundred for you. And we need to do it right. We're scheduled to do it Wednesday, but I want to do it today. We got to prepare good for this one. This doctor in Drain is the bookkeeper and banker for the car-theft ring part of this operation. He keeps the money, and he also does all the bullet removals, operations, plastic surgery, and all that. We've got to come up with some kind of inventive way to get in his house with him there, so he can open the safe for us. He's got a maid that stays at his house all day, so it will have to be at night. He takes his retarded son to baseball games every Monday and Wednesday afternoon, drops him off, then picks him up. I've got a general plan."

Henry noticed a tone he hadn't heard before — something that sounded a little bit like being scared of something. The plantation safe had been fun, hadn't it? They'd had to improvise. Maybe Clearwater didn't like that part. He seemed different. He'd always seemed bigger than life. Now he seemed not quite so big.

"What'll it be after that?" asked Henry.

"A vacation. You can buy a car, go see your girlfriend. Leave me a phone number up in North Carolina and I'll call you in a week or two."

They talked through their plan, stopped for lunch and then at a clothing store to shop for Henry's disguise. He was going to have to dress up like a girl.

In the early afternoon, they arrived in Drain and Henry pulled over and got out of the car a hundred yards prior to a motel with a small palm tree beside a neon sign, BULLOCK'S MOTEL, FREE SHOWER AND TV. A neon rooster hung in the window — red, blue, and yellow.

They were to meet in Clearwater's room before Clearwater went to the ball game, where the doctor and his son would be.

Henry tapped on the door and Clearwater unlocked it. In the room was a bed, table, two chairs, a television — like Henry's, except Clearwater's bedspread was green instead of brown.

"Does your TV work?" asked Henry.

"I ain't interested in it. We got to talk over a couple of things before this gig."

Henry noticed Clearwater's canvas bag and other things against a wall. On the table was an open road map, two hand-drawn maps, and a grocery sack full of his disguise. Clearwater sat leaning back against the headboard, two pillows behind him, his legs stretched across the bed. He was wearing thin black socks.

"Have a seat. There beside the maps. When we finish up tomorrow night, I'll be taking his car because we already know it's stolen, and you follow me south out of town and keep that way, or west then around to south, or north then south." Henry looked on the big road map for a northeasterly route. Route 71. Didn't 71 lead up to . . . yes, Jeffries.

"What the hell are you looking at?" said Clearwater.

"The map."

"You just need what I drew on there. And be a girl that don't talk. Get the clothes outen that bag. It should all go pretty smooth. He'll open the safe and give us what's in there. I'll turn it over to the FBI. Questions?"

"I can't think of any."

"I'll be back in about an hour or two. You wait here."

Just after the ball game was over, Clearwater caught up with the doctor and his son at the doctor's car, introduced himself as Major Frank Arnold, retired, and after a short, friendly conversation explained quietly that his niece, Roberta, was pregnant by either her father or a cousin — or an uncle. She needed an abortion as soon as possible. He could pay more than top dollar.

The doctor told Major Arnold where he lived and said to bring Roberta to his house that night at eleven. He said that they could park behind a church two houses down and follow the back alleyway.

Wearing the dress, wig, hat, and makeup, Henry walked along the alleyway toward the doctor's house. His throat was terribly dry. Something was wrong.

Ten minutes earlier he had been loading his stuff into the Chrysler trunk. There lay a brand-new car jack with a tag taped onto it: Chrysler Sales, Drain, Georgia. The tape placement — across the sprockets — showed the jack hadn't been used. But the spare tire . . . it was not new like it had been. What? He walked around the car. The white sidewall, front right, was slightly green — brand-new: the spare! But they hadn't had a flat. A realization began . . . a series . . .

Clearwater, carrying his canvas bag, walked beside Henry. Henry had not spoken. He was not supposed to. He wasn't sure if he could. Fireflies blinked off and on along the dark alleyway and in the backyards of fine large homes.

A series of memories had plopped into an order like the reversed film of a building collapsing: The brand-new car jack. The spare tire now on the car. Mrs. Finley's story about the murder and the car jack. Clearwater taking something into the woods that night, after saying he was going to the truck stop for a drink.

Clearwater pushed open a tall metal gate. Off to the side stood a two-story garage with a light over the door shining down onto the car Henry knew they were supposed to take — a cream-colored Cadillac, facing the garage. He could run, but Clearwater probably had a gun.

"There's the car," said Clearwater. "You drive the Chrysler, remember."

On the screened-in back porch Clearwater pushed a doorbell button, and from inside came a sound like a telephone ring. Henry looked around. Against a wall was a porch swing that hadn't been hung. Against another wall were several cardboard boxes with green pineapples printed on the side. Should he just charge off the porch? No. He'd wait for a better chance to run.

The door opened and a man stood dressed in a white jacket with a stethoscope in the front pocket. He held a cup of coffee or something that released a trace of steam. "Come in, Major. Roberta."

"Doctor," said Clearwater. "How you doing?"

"Fine. Come right in."

"She don't talk much," said Clearwater, "but she's got a real sweet disposition. I got some of her things here in the bag."

"Come through to my study," said the doctor. They were

in a large kitchen with counters and cabinets all the way around. Henry noticed a toaster, big and silver, that plugged into the wall, and there was a coffeepot that had an electric cord. *Where could he run to? He had to think. Think very clearly, slowly. Get it right.* They walked through a breakfast room, a sitting room, and a living room, and then into a study with books lining the walls. The room looked like an expensive hotel lobby. On a coffee table in front of a leather couch sat a beveled glass pitcher of ice water and two glasses.

"Have a seat there on the couch and have a drink of water if you like," said the doctor. He sat in a big leather chair across from the couch. "I'll explain the procedure."

Clearwater leaned forward, opened his canvas bag, pulled out his snub-nosed .38, and pointed it at the doctor. "We won't be needing any explaining, Doctor. But we do need you to open your safe, and we'd like you to do that as quickly as possible."

"Is this a joke?" asked the doctor. His face held a half smile but also a look of new knowledge.

"No, it's not a joke," said Clearwater.

A door opened behind Henry.

Clearwater bolted up and moved to where he could see everybody at once.

It was the son.

"Get back in your room, Randy," said the doctor.

Randy was dressed in blue pajamas and wore a denim jacket with Sunday school attendance medals and men's service club buttons — Elks, Sertoma, Moose. His round face sat on wide shoulders, his brown hair was cropped short, his mouth hung open. He held a teddy bear. He was trying to talk.

Henry thought of Yancy. When he saw that Randy was coming for him, he stood, stepped over the coffee table, stopped between the doctor and Clearwater. Randy kept coming, his brown eyes open wide in surprise and delight.

"Get back in your room, I said," said the doctor.

Clearwater moved again — to cover the doctor. He watched as Randy gripped a large quantity of cloth on a sleeve of Henry's dress. Randy was smiling and making grunting noises.

"Sometimes he's difficult," said the doctor.

"This would be a bad time for that," said Clearwater. "Just stand there and be still," he said to Henry. "Let him hold your sleeve. And sir, you need to open your safe right away."

"Turn me loose," Henry said to Randy.

"You be quiet," snapped Clearwater.

The doctor, still seated, said, "Randy, you behave yourself. Major Arnold, I don't have a safe."

"I think you do. You don't bank anywhere around here."

"I invest my money in stocks."

"Stocks?"

"My maid delivers all my cash to a financial adviser every Friday. There is no safe, sir. I can show you the paperwork, the stock market paperwork, in my top desk drawer over there." He stood.

"Sit back down!" And then to Henry: "And you sit down on the couch." He motioned with the gun.

Henry was down in something too deep to see out of. And this Randy wouldn't turn loose his sleeve.

With Randy attached, Henry moved back around the coffee table and sat. Randy stood, holding Henry's arm, which was raised as if Henry had a question for a teacher.

"There is no safe," said the doctor. "And I'm expecting another patient." He looked at his watch. "Before long."

"Well, you work too fast." Then to Henry: "Go get some pillowcases. Anything that will hold money."

"He's holding on to me."

"Take him with you," said Clearwater. "Back in there where he came out of."

Henry walked, with Randy holding on, into a bedroom. He gathered two pillowcases and a laundry bag and returned to the study. Randy held to his dress sleeve.

Clearwater said, "Go get the Chrysler and bring it up to the gate."

"He won't turn loose."

"Get rid of him."

"Where's the keys?" said Henry.

"There's a set under the floor mat."

When Henry and Randy got to the back door, Henry saw car keys on a nail. *The Cadillac.* He got them. With Randy attached, he opened the back door to the warm night; onto the back porch, through the screen door. He realized he'd picked up Clearwater's canvas bag.

"Oroof," Randy said. He turned loose Henry's sleeve.

Henry looked at the car keys in his hand, headed toward

the driver's door, slipped in behind the steering wheel, dropped the bag onto the seat beside him.

Randy was opening the passenger door.

"Don't get in," said Henry.

Randy got in anyway.

Henry thought about getting out, then started the engine, turned on the headlights, backed into the alley, drove past the Chrysler, stopped, backed up. He wanted his stuff. He found the Chrysler keys, opened the trunk, loaded his suitcase and valise into the backseat of the Cadillac, got back behind the steering wheel, pulled onto the street.

The plan was to circle south and head north, but he needed to head northeast — on 71.

The car jack. He needed to think that through again. He needed to get rid of that canvas bag, didn't he? Why? Why should he keep it? The bad guys would know Clearwater had been undercover. Was he undercover? No. He'd been stealing all along. And Henry had too. Clearwater murdered a man. Maybe the man was a criminal. What if that was it? Who was Blinky? If the truck driver was a criminal, Clearwater would not have buried that car jack.

In the doctor's house, Clearwater was feeling things fall apart. He was going to have to kidnap the son of a bitch. A patient would be there at midnight, with her mother and father. He'd seen the appointment book. The doctor had pulled it from his pocket and handed it to him. On the back porch, standing behind the doctor, Clearwater looked for the Chrysler at the gate. It wasn't there, and the Cadillac . . . was . . . What had happened flashed into his brain, and he awaited the full realization like waiting for the sound of a giant tree that had just fallen far across a field.

The doctor called out, "Randy. Randy?"

"Walk through that gate, Doctor," said Clearwater. "I need to chase down that son of a bitch Bible salesman. He's on Seventy-one north. I can't let him loose on the world."

Henry remembered that to get on Highway 71 he'd have to cross the railroad track on Main Street, drive along beside it, then cross the track a second time. There. Yes. The sign said he was on 71. What could he tell Marleen? He had to get to her. It was a right long ways. He could stop at a police station. He pressed on the gas pedal. He glanced at Randy, sitting with his arms between his legs.

Then he knew exactly what he had to do. He had to go back.

No, he didn't. He'd keep going until the next town. He'd go straight to the police station. He watched the needle go past seventy on a straightaway. He slowed for a curve. He couldn't remember how far he had to go before the next town. He wanted to go home. He had to get back into Drain and call the police. Of course. That was the thing to do. He could not lose. They would contact the FBI and everything would be good. They might even give him a job for sure.

He turned onto a dirt road and stopped. What if the car-theft gang came after him? That's who Clearwater was with all along. He needed to get rid of the canvas bag. He reached for it, felt something hard in there, in the bag — sure enough. He unzipped the bag and reached in. A jacket and . . . a pistol. Would he *need* it? The bad guys wouldn't mess around. Maybe Clearwater *was* with the FBI. What if he *was?* "Dear Jesus," he prayed. "Guide and direct me." He'd keep the gun under his belt. He still had on the dress. He walked into the woods a ways with the bag and dropped it. What about Randy? One thing at a time. He remembered Carson always carrying two guns in his belt when they played cowboys and Indians. He remembered wanting to be an Indian.

Back in the car, headed back to Drain, he pressed the gas pedal, watched the needle move to sixty, turned the radio dial, and stopped it on a station where he heard a familiar sound. "Do you know who that is?" he asked Randy. He would just talk for a minute.

Randy looked at him and then at the radio.

"That's Hank Williams. 'Why Don't You Love Me.'"

They were in a curve to the right — drifting over the middle line — when headlights appeared as if risen from the ground. Henry swerved right but couldn't avoid the sideswipe, ricocheting off the Cadillac like a glancing billiard ball. He saw the ditch coming and, as he stomped the brakes, heard a loud, earth-shaking thud-bang behind him somewhere — the other car hitting something.

His door did not open easily, but he got it open and stood on the asphalt. His heart was racing. He had to leave quickly. No, help out. The *police* would be here, right away. A bright moon lit the road in both directions. Back down the road, a lone headlight was shining from the car that had hit the tree — shining upward at a sick angle like a spotlight, smoke and dust drifting through the beam. He unbuttoned and stepped from the dress and threw it toward the ditch. He should go help out. That's what he had to do. "Do unto others as you would have them . . ." It looked like . . . he believed it was a Chrysler. Could it . . . ?

He opened the back door of the Cadillac and grabbed his suitcase and valise. Randy's door was against the ditch bank, and Randy was slowly sliding across the front seat toward the steering wheel. Henry looked at the other car again. Somebody was getting out of the driver's side. Oh God, yes, it was Clearwater, holding his head. Oh God. Henry jumped the ditch, started walking toward the woods. Something pulled him toward the Chrysler. He would say, "That was a close call. Are you okay?"

But he ran into the woods. What would Randy do? He really didn't know Randy. They were not friends. He'd just met him. Henry's foot, leg — a hole. He stumbled, fell, felt for the pistol. It was still there, under his belt. He got up, found his suitcase and valise. He would keep going as far and fast as he could. A loud pop. A gunshot? What in the world? Clearwater wouldn't . . . What happened back there? After a few minutes of catching his pants in briars, stumbling, almost falling, he burst into a field, his throat dry. He looked straight ahead, over a distant line of woods and up into the full bright moon that bore into him like a lone headlight. He found a tree, sat down, leaned his back against it, and looked up at a gray-white cloud skittering along, lit from behind.

He heard somebody coming. Randy? I'll just sit still, he thought. Wait, and let him go by me.

He looked back toward the sounds. Where the hell did he get a flashlight? Was that Randy? Oh, no . . . He slipped on his butt to the side of the tree away from the flashlight, now shining here and there as if lighting up the entire woods. He pulled out the pistol, cocked it, held it in his hand under his leg. The flashlight was beside him, then in front of him, shining in his eyes, right there in front of him so that he could see nothing behind the light.

"You made a big mistake." Clearwater's voice, garbled somehow. "You're dead, sonny."

"You won't in the FBI, were you?"

"I said you are dead."

A kind of wordless message flashed before Henry: *Love him and die. Kill him and live.* "I was coming back for you," he said. *Improvise.* "I just heard this Hank Williams song and I was thinking about what it was like, you playing music with that fellow you knew in Knoxville. Sit on that stump right there and tell me. I forgot his name. Just tell me his name, something about him."

Clearwater knew something was wrong with his neck, head, and leg. His sock, the right one, felt sticky and wet — blood — and he had to sit down, but he needed to kill the boy because he knew too much and had *double-crossed* him. His chin was tingling. He looked into the face shining up at him, the pale face, makeup, and lipstick. "Roy Acuff," he said, and turned his head to look for that stump.

Henry raised his gun and pulled the trigger, saw both flashes, heard two shots — his and one from Clearwater's gun — and felt a bullet slam into the tree beside his ear as if he'd shot at himself. Henry fired three more times: bam, bam, bam. Clearwater collapsed onto the ground with a low moaning. He lay on his back, his leg moving.

The leg stopped moving.

Henry stood. He looked over his shoulder. He started to walk away and then walked back, looked at the body again. He bent over and picked up Clearwater's left arm and then let it drop. The right hand held the pistol. He needed to move it out of his hand. What if he wasn't dead?

Henry's knees were shaking. He felt nauseated. Far through the trees he saw light from the headlight beam. Without turning, he experienced a yawning of the woods behind him, a great yawning out of which came a vacuum, and to Henry its color was yellow and it was more clear and definite and real than Jesus had been when Henry used to pray to him and *see* him. He was on his own now. Certainty had birthed an uncertainty.

He knelt and removed the gun from Clearwater's hand. It came easily. He didn't want it there to shoot him as he walked away. He threw it as far as he could. He had to tell somebody. The sound of the gunshots was in his head.

Stop and just think. The doctor would tell the police he didn't do anything. The doctor would be on his side. The next car that came by out there would stop, probably. But there was no traffic. They must be in the middle of nowhere. He wanted to go home.

He heard something coming, rustling along. Randy? Had Clearwater brought the doctor? Or had he . . .

He stepped behind a tree. He could hide, then walk along the road. He had to go home. His valise and suitcase! Where were they? His money was in the suitcase. It was Randy coming. But his money was in his suitcase. He stepped out. "Hey," he said.

Randy stopped, looked at Henry, and turned halfway around.

"Wait," said Henry. "Stand right there. I got to go back just a little ways and get my suitcase and valise. Wait right there." Randy acted as if he did not know him. Oh. He wasn't in the dress. He'd left it by the ditch. And where was the wig? He walked back to the tree, found his suitcase and valise. Then Randy followed him as he trudged back toward the road. Henry didn't know what to say to Randy. His face felt numb. He finally got to the Chrysler, looked in the back window, walked to the other side of the car, and there he saw the doctor on the ground, sprawled faceup, a bullet hole in his forehead. "Stay over there in the road," he said to Randy. "We got to start walking now."

Mrs. Albright was awakened late Tuesday night by a knock on the front door. She slipped on an old shirt of Yancy's, turned on the bedroom light, the living room light, the front porch light, and then opened the front door.

He wore a denim jacket with pin-on buttons. He stood there, not speaking.

"You look . . . you look familiar," she said. Somebody was driving away. "Come in the house, young man. Come in."

The young man bent, reached toward a cat, then looked up at Mrs. Albright.

"Yancy?" she asked. "Is it you, Yancy? You like cats now? Oh, Yancy. Jesus has raised you and sent you home. Let me fix you something to eat, son. Come on in here and sit down at your place. Nobody will believe this. Nobody will believe me." He reached out to her, took hold of her sleeve.

Thomas's tail tip moved as if it were alive. He stood and followed the old lady and the new man. Several other cats came along. Angel said, "Glory hallelujah! I'm going to pour me a little drink. This is too good to be true." Isaac said, "Listen. Hear the rats out back?"

Mrs. Albright opened the back door. "Go catch you one," she said. Several cats scooted out. Then she looked into Randy's face and smiled. He stood, holding on to her sleeve.

"Why don't you sit down right here?" she said. "I'll fix you a bite to eat."

Henry drove around for an hour — in the '39 Ford coupe he'd paid cash for just outside Drain — then drove down to Swan Island and checked into the Deluxe Olympia Hotel. It was two a.m. His mind replayed the last two days, the last few months. He lay on his bed unable to sleep. He was dizzy with fatigue. He had to tell. He called the police station.

The McNeill police car pulled up in front of the Deluxe, and officer Donald Sturgis opened the car door, stood behind it a minute looking around, hitched his belt, walked inside to Henry's room, and knocked.

Sturgis sat in a chair. Henry talked. Sturgis listened, then said, "Come on with me down to the station."

At the station, Henry sat in a chair in Chief Bob Hillman's office and talked again. Chief Hillman called Sturgis in to sit with Henry, then walked out, stayed gone for a while, walked back in, sat down.

"Mr. Dampier," said the chief, "I hate to get waked up in the middle of the night for malarkey like this. I've talked to the police in Drain. Just now. On the phone. There was no Preston Clearwater involved. The man shot in the woods down there was Gregory Vinson, and he's been identified by his family. He's a war hero. You must have heard about this on the radio. That they know who murdered him — and that doctor. The Night Shooter. And they've arrested a colored boy in Brownlee for shooting that truck driver. I made that phone call too. Officer Sturgis didn't think to make these phone calls before he called me in the middle of the night. And on top of that, Mr." — he looked at his notepad — "Dampier, nobody reported a safe stole down in Panakala. I made that call too. And if you think Blinky — Mr. Smathers — at Johnson and Ball is a criminal, then you got another thought coming. I'm not calling him in the middle of the night. Sturgis, take this fellow back where he came from. And for God's sake learn to use the damn telephone, Sturgis. And listen, son, you go on home and don't be playing no more tricks like this."

*   *   *

At the homeplace the next morning, Henry told Aunt Dorie he had to finish up something he was in the middle of. "I'll be gone a couple of days and then I'll call you."

"Henry, you look terrible. You need to go to bed. What's wrong?"

"I'll be back as soon as I can."

"Do you have to go out again right now?"

"Yes ma'am. I do."

"Well here, take this, son. I cleared yours and Carson's little things off the dresser and put them in the top drawer, and I knew which of all the things were yours, and so I wrote them down for some reason. Right here. Here, take this with you."

"Okay. Bye. I'll be back. I love you. I'm sorry."

"I love you."

In his car, before cranking it, he read:

necktie clip, package of bbs, wooden gun, an old pocket watch with tiny wheels out and lying around, knife in holster, piece of leather about 15 inches long, small corncob pipe, 2 Bibles, map, box of 20 gauge gun shells, 2 pocket knives, eleven penny prizes, world globe, Tom Mix billfold, piece of broken glass, rubber bands, Sunday school quarterly, small cedar chest, old army overseas cap, tin box full of marbles, broken field glasses with one lens missing, 12 inch ruler, 2 keys, 2 pencils, one broken marionette head and sandpaper,

tract on tithing, book of rules for carom, leather
watch band, toy airplane

He drove down to Mrs. Albright's. He'd decided that the
only way he'd get listened to by any kind of officials was to
take Randy back to Drain. He walked up onto the porch and
knocked. Mrs. Albright opened the door, spread her arms.
"Oh, Henry. Henry, a miracle has happened. I thought it was
Yancy at first, but it's somebody new that has returned in his
place. I don't know how it happened. Come on in." She
stepped back for him to enter. "Somebody dropped him off.
Look. It's a miracle."

Randy sat in the middle of the living room floor. He wore
Yancy's clothes. The electric train was running its orbit.

"I've been calling him Jericho," said Mrs. Albright. "All
the horns and trumpets they blowed and all. I haven't even
told nobody that he's here. You're the first person to come
by. Sit down. He loves the cats."

Henry settled into a chair, breathed in, out, looked
around. His eyes felt full of sand. "Mrs. Albright, this is
hard. I'm in the middle of something I'm trying to solve. I
need to take . . . his name is Randy, and I'm the one brought
him here yesterday, or day before, whenever it was, and I
made a big mistake and I need to take him back to prove that
I was involved in some stuff I need to own up to, or straighten
out somehow. I'm the only one can do it."

Mrs. Albright turned to stone. But her eyes, alive, stayed
on Henry's eyes as if they were in them.

"Well, then," said Henry. "Let me think of something else. I can think of something else, I guess."

In Henry's old desk at the homeplace was a Kodak box camera and a roll of film. He found them. Aunt Dorie followed him back outside. "Can't you tell me anything?" she asked.

"I can, as soon as I get things straight. I've got a girlfriend. I can tell you that. But I've gotten into trouble in a way, not in any way you can imagine. Everything is okay, but it's not. I can explain, but I've got to send a picture to Georgia first."

"Henry, I miss you so much. I hope you haven't been drifting from God."

"I'm not drifting."

"Can Carson help you out?"

"I'll go see him, but I've got to work this out on my own."

Over a week later, the Atlanta police received a photograph of the missing Criddenton boy and a woman identified — in a long letter from a Henry Dampier — as Mrs. John Albright.

Linda Abbott, a social worker from Drain who worked in Atlanta, and Detective Smithy Newman were assigned the case. Mrs. Abbott was familiar with the Criddenton situation: the doctor, the retarded boy, the mother who disappeared years earlier. She knew the facts not from her social work, but from town knowledge.

She and Detective Newman decided to visit Simmons,

North Carolina. Mrs. Abbott would visit Mrs. Albright, and Newman would meet with the Dampier boy.

Mrs. Abbott's preliminary report suggested that the Criddenton boy stay where he was. She could imagine no better place for him, and there were no relatives to insist otherwise. She would be willing to arrange for guardianship.

Newman investigated possible charges against Henry and then refused to bring any, given a lack of evidence of criminal intent. Investigations of a car-theft ring operating out of McNeill, North Carolina, and a murder in Brownlee, Georgia, were begun.

1951

For their honeymoon, Henry and Marleen spent two nights and a day at the Deluxe Olympia Hotel and then drove up the coast to catch the three-car ferry at Tiny Bob's Crossing for a two-day fishing and camping stay on Mc-Garren Island. They left the Ford on the mainland — they were walk-ons — and had with them a tent, two fold-up beach chairs, fishing gear, cast net, a cooler of drinks, groceries, paper plates, and a skillet. They stacked their belongings against the back of the pilot house near the bow of the ferry. Two old Buicks with extra-wide, half-flat tires were the main cargo.

"Do you know what's biting over there?" asked one of the car owners. He wore a white sweatshirt, blue shorts, and shoes without socks.

"No idea," said Henry. "Does that Buick go pretty well on the sand?"

"Better than a lot of jeeps. You planning on doing some reading?"

"Yeah, maybe." Henry held up the book in his hand. It didn't look like a Bible — more like a hardback novel. It was a wedding gift, sent from his Bible-selling teacher, Mr. Fletcher, *The Bible: An American Translation*. In his note that came with it, Mr. Fletcher called it the Chicago Bible, because it had been translated up there. He said he was sorry to miss the wedding and he appreciated his invite.

Once he and Marleen set up camp near the southern end of the island, Henry walked with the cast net and a bucket over to the sound side. He hauled in enough finger mullet for the afternoon's fishing.

There wasn't much that Henry could teach Marleen about surf fishing. She'd fished in Georgia, knew how to cast, and had read about it after they decided where to honeymoon.

They sat in their wood-and-cloth beach chairs and watched the tips of their rods. The rods rested in metal pole holders stuck in the sand. It was turning cool enough for both of them to wear long pants and long-sleeved shirts.

Nothing was biting, so they talked. Henry had brought along his new Bible. He'd been reading it like a novel, telling Marleen how it was different from the one he grew up with.

"Why don't you order some free ones and give them away? How many of the others did you give away?"

"I lost count. I doubt I could get the Chicago ones. You remember I told you about Trixie's Bible that Uncle Jack used to talk about — there are no miracles; nobody can see into the future? Listen to this, especially the last sentence. It's from Ecclesiastes. I can't get over it." He read:

For there is one fate for both man and beast — the same fate for them; as the one dies, so dies the other; the same breath is in all of them, and man has no advantage over the beast; for everything is futility. All go to one place; all are from the dust, and all return to the dust. Who knows whether the spirit of men goes upward and the spirit of the beast goes downward to the earth? And I saw that there is nothing better than that man should rejoice in his work, since that is his portion; for who can bring him to see what shall be after him?

"I used to believe," said Henry, "that that would be *God's* word because it's in the Bible. Maybe it is. But it's David's son talking."

"Are you going to read that to Aunt Dorie?"

"I might."

"Why not — it's in the Bible."

"Everything is in there. I don't know what I can say to Aunt Dorie. Well, I'll tell her I believe in hope and fear — the things the fiddle player at Indian Springs said. You know. But that's kind of general, until you start talking about something specific."

"I want you to take me to Indian Springs."

"I will. I promise," said Henry.

"Let's go there next year for our first anniversary. Remember when I wondered what we'd be doing in a year — last year this time?"

"Oh yeah. That was a bad time. Mr. Clearwater. Do you remember having any thoughts about what he was up to that one time you saw him?"

"I thought he looked businesslike. Handsome. Nice. Kind of big ears, but not too big, I guess."

"He did look a little like Clark Gable."

"I didn't see that."

"Look! You got a bite. Get him."

The rod tip was bending forward, springing back, bending forward. Marleen jumped from her chair. She grabbed her rod, reeled in a two-and-a-half-pound redfish, took it off the hook, admired it, dropped it into their bucket.

They settled back in their chairs.

"Where were we?" asked Henry. "Oh, on Clearwater."

"He didn't look like a bad person."

"Let's talk about something else."

"What should we name our first child?" asked Marleen.

"You been thinking about that?"

"First, if it's a boy. Two names. I pick one. You pick one."

"Danny," said Henry.

"Howard, my daddy."

"Or maybe Jack."

"I'm glad we're going to see him finally," said Marleen.

"You'll like him. He really wants to meet you."

"What about a girl?" said Marleen.

"Ah, I guess Dorie, or maybe Ruth or . . . I don't know."

"Tressie," said Marleen. "Tressie Ruth would be good. What about Henry Junior?"

"I don't think so. Two Juniors would be too much. Have you noticed that Glenn Junior's looking more and more like Mr. Clearwater?"

"You're sure about all that?"

"Sure as blood."

"He does have big ears."

"I know Caroline sees it, and she's going to know that I see it, and she'll have to bring it up. She asked after Mr. Clearwater when I came home last summer — and she was calling him Preston instead of Mr. Clearwater. That should have told me something."

"Why don't you bring it up to her?"

"I couldn't. I wouldn't know what to say. Maybe she'll tell you."

"When I get pregnant we'll have some good talks, I'll bet."

They headed to their tent as the bright low sun slowly dropped toward the long line of trees far across the Pamlico Sound.

"Look," said Henry. "Look how far my hand shadow goes down the beach. In a minute it'll go on across the sand and then onto the water and then on out into outer space."

"I never thought about that," said Marleen. "Let's do it. Let's both do it."

They each held up a hand, standing there near the southern tip of the island, their backs to the sun setting over McGarren Sound, their shadows lengthening across the sand, then out onto the ocean.

"It'll be our whole bodies," said Marleen. "Our whole bodies blocking a speck of sunlight from outer space, and . . . and if you could travel as fast as light, then you could get right out there in space a little ways and then you could see us standing here together for . . . how many light-years is it across the whole universe?"

"Two hundred billion. I have no idea."

"Let's look it up. Maybe nobody knows. But that's how long our shadows will be out there — together."

"That's a long time."

"Almost forever," said Marleen.

"'And I will dwell in the house of the LORD for ever.' I wonder if the Twenty-third Psalm is any different in the Chicago Bible."

They built a campfire, and Henry filleted and fried their redfish, served it with sliced apples and loaf bread. After dark, and more talking, they settled in the tent. With a flashlight, Henry looked for the "house of the LORD for ever" at the end of the Twenty-third Psalm, the way he'd always seen it.

The LORD is my shepherd; I shall not want;
In green meadows he makes me lie down;
Beside refreshing waters he leads me.
He gives me new life;

He guides me in paths of righteousness, for his name's
      sake.
Even though I walk in the darkest valley,
I fear no harm; for thou art with me;
Thy rod and thy staff — they comfort me.
Thou layest a table before me in the presence of my
      enemies;
Thou anointest my head with oil; my cup overflows.
Surely goodness and kindness shall follow me all the
      days of my life;
And I shall dwell in the house of the LORD to an old age.

"Marleen, *listen*." He read the entire psalm to her. "That last sentence has got some meat on it."

They talked more after getting into their sleeping bags. In a while, Marleen invited Henry into hers. After the magic, and after Henry was back in his own sleeping bag, they talked about the end of the world, the atomic bomb, and how the Bible talked about fire at the end. Henry said it would be fire or water probably, and one fifty-percent guess was as good as another.

They were quiet for a while. Henry said, "Had you rather burn up or drown?"

"Let's don't talk about that."

"Okay."

They lay there awhile. The wind was up a little.

"Let's sleep outside," said Marleen. "And imagine our shadows flying together through space."

While she smoothed out her spot in the sand, Henry smoothed out a spot for his sleeping bag, put it down, wiped the sand off his feet, and crawled in and lay on his back.

"Come over and get in with me for just a minute or two," she said.

"Okay."

No moon, no lights, clear sky, the waves so regular as to be hardly noticed — and the sky so bright with stars, scattered like sand thrown up by the handfuls.

"It feels like we're moving through space with the ground slipped out from under us," said Henry.

Acknowledgments

For advice and support, I thank Pat Strachan, Liz Darhansoff, Peter Workman, Peggy Leith Anderson, and Shannon Ravenel. For suggestions, stories, and other support, thanks to Louis Rubin, Hilbert Campbell, Robert Siegel, Sterling Hennis, Sharon Boyd, Kristina Edgerton, Tom Rankin, Billy Ray Brown, John Justice, Captain Mark Batson (safe and vault acquisition and security), Jim Watson, Catherine Edgerton, David McGirt, Nancy McGirt, Yvonne Mason, Clifford Swain, Buddy Swain, Joe Mann, Mike Craver, Lewis Nordan, June Highfill, George Singleton, John Hart, Buster Quin, Jan Henley, George Terll, P. M. Jones, Hannah Jones, John Penick, Zama Dexter, Bobbie Hicks, Johnnye Lott, Roseanne Osborne, Dr. Larry M. Taylor, and the woman at a November 19, 2006, fund-raiser for the North Carolina Council of Churches who told me a story about a red dress and a funeral.

Particularly helpful and inspirational during the creation of this story were several nonfiction narratives — in particular *Jesus and Yahweh: The Names Divine,* by Harold Bloom; *Beasts, Horns, and the Antichrist,* by Broderick D. Shepherd; and *The Story of the New Testament,* by Edgar Goodspeed.

ABOUT THE AUTHOR

CLYDE EDGERTON was born in Durham, North Carolina. He is the author of eight previous novels, including *Walking Across Egypt* and *Lunch at the Piccadilly*. He has been a Guggenheim Fellow, and five of his novels have been *New York Times* Notable Books. Edgerton teaches creative writing at the University of North Carolina Wilmington. He lives in Wilmington with his wife, Kristina, and their children.